Roberto Bolaño

The Insufferable Gaucho

TRANSLATED BY CHRIS ANDREWS

Roberto Bolaño (1953–2003) was the author of *The Savage Detectives* and *2666*, among many other notable works. Born in Santiago, Chile, he later lived in Mexico City, Paris, and Barcelona. His accolades include the National Book Critics Circle Award and the Premio Rómulo Gallegos. He died at the age of fifty and is widely considered to be the greatest Latin American writer of his generation.

Chris Andrews has translated books of prose fiction by César Aira, Roberto Bolaño, Liliana Colanzi, and Ágota Kristóf, among others. He is also the author of *How to Do Things with Forms* and *The Oblong Plot*.

Also by Roberto Bolaño

Cowboy Graves

The Spirit of Science Fiction

A Little Lumpen Novelita

The Unknown University

Woes of the True Policeman

The Third Reich

Tres

The Return

Antwerp

Monsieur Pain

The Skating Rink

The Romantic Dogs

2666

Nazi Literature in the Americas

The Savage Detectives

Amulet

Last Evenings on Earth

Distant Star

By Night in Chile

Roberto Bolaño

The Insufferable Gaucho

Translated from the Spanish by
CHRIS ANDREWS

Picador • New York

Picador
120 Broadway, New York 10271

Copyright © 2003 by the Heirs of Roberto Bolaño
Translation copyright © 2010 by Chris Andrews
All rights reserved
Printed in the United States of America
Originally published in 2003 by Editorial Anagrama, Spain, as *El gaucho insufrible*
English translation originally published in 2010 by New Directions, by arrangement with the Heirs of Roberto Bolaño and Carmen Balcells Agencia Literaria, Barcelona
First Picador paperback edition, 2025

Owing to limitations of space, all acknowledgments for permission to reprint previously published material can be found on page 165.

Library of Congress Cataloging-in-Publication Data
Names: Bolaño, Roberto, 1953–2003, author. | Andrews, Chris, 1962– translator.
Title: The insufferable gaucho / Roberto Bolaño ; translated by Chris Andrews.
Other titles: El gaucho insufrible. English
Description: First Picador paperback edition. | New York : Picador, 2025. | "Originally published in 2003 by Editorial Anagrama, Spain, as El gaucho insufrible. English translation originally published in 2010 by New Directions"—Title page verso.
Identifiers: LCCN 2024034084 | ISBN 9781250898203 (paperback)
Subjects: LCGFT: Short stories. | Essays.
Classification: LCC PQ8098.12.O38 G3813 2025 | DDC 863/.64—dc23/eng/20240724
LC record available at https://lccn.loc.gov/2024034084

Our books may be purchased in bulk for promotional, educational, or business use. Please contact your local bookseller or the Macmillan Corporate and Premium Sales Department at 1-800-221-7945, extension 5442, or by email at MacmillanSpecialMarkets@macmillan.com.

Picador® is a U.S. registered trademark and is used by Macmillan Publishing Group, LLC, under license from Pan Books Limited.

For book club information, please email marketing@picadorusa.com.

picadorusa.com • Follow us on social media at @picador or @picadorusa

10 9 8 7 6 5 4 3 2 1

For my children Lautaro and Alexandra
and for my friend Ignacio Echevarría

So perhaps we shall not miss so very much after all.

—Franz Kafka

CONTENTS

JIM

Many years ago I had a friend named Jim, and he was the saddest North American I've ever come across. I've seen a lot of desperate men. But never one as sad as Jim. Once he went to Peru—supposedly for more than six months, but it wasn't long before I saw him again. The Mexican street kids used to ask him, What's poetry made of, Jim? Listening to them, Jim would stare at the clouds and then he'd start throwing up. Vocabulary, eloquence, the search for truth. Epiphany. Like when you have a vision of the Virgin. He was mugged several times in Central America, which is surprising, because he'd been a marine and fought in Vietnam. No more fighting, Jim used to say. I'm a poet now, searching for the extraordinary, trying to express it in ordinary, everyday words. So you think there are ordinary, everyday words? I think there are, Jim used to say. His wife was a Chicana poet; every so often she'd threaten to leave him. He showed me a photo of her. She wasn't especially pretty. Her face betrayed suffering, and under that suffering, simmering rage. I imagined her in an apartment in San Francisco or a house in Los Angeles, with the windows shut and the curtains open, sitting at a table, eating sliced bread and a bowl of green soup. Jim liked dark women, apparently, history's secret women, he would say, without elaborating. As for me, I liked blondes. Once I saw him watching fire-eaters on a street in Mexico City. I saw him from behind, and I didn't say hello, but it was obviously Jim. The badly cut hair, the dirty white shirt and the stoop, as if he were still weighed down by his pack. Somehow his neck, his red neck, summoned up the image of a lynching in the country—a landscape in black and white, without billboards or gas station lights—the country as it is or ought to be: one expanse of idle land blurring into the next, brick-walled rooms or bunkers from which we have escaped, standing there, awaiting our return. Jim had his hands in his pockets. The fire-eater was waving his torch and laughing fiercely. His blackened face was ageless: he could have been thirty-five or fifteen. He wasn't wearing a shirt and there was a vertical scar from his navel to his breastbone. Every so often he'd fill his mouth with flammable liquid and spit out a long snake of fire. The people in the street would watch him for a while, admire his skill, and continue on their way, except for Jim, who remained there on the edge of the sidewalk, stock-still, as if he expected something more from the fire-eater, a tenth signal (having deciphered the usual nine), or as if he'd seen in that discolored face the features of an old friend or of someone he'd killed. I watched him for a good long while. I was eighteen or nineteen at the time and believed I was immortal. If I'd realized that I wasn't, I would have turned around and walked away. After a while I got tired of looking at Jim's back and the fire-eater's grimaces. So I went over and called his name. Jim didn't seem to hear me. When he turned around

I noticed that his face was covered with sweat. He seemed to be feverish, and it took him a while to work out who I was; he greeted me with a nod and then turned back to the fire-eater. Standing beside him, I noticed he was crying. He probably had a fever as well. I also discovered something that surprised me less at the time than it does now, writing this: the fire-eater was performing exclusively for Jim, as if all the other passersby on that corner in Mexico City simply didn't exist. Sometimes the flames came within a yard of where we were standing. What are you waiting for, I said, you want to get barbecued in the street? It was a stupid wisecrack, I said it without thinking, but then it hit me: that's exactly what Jim's waiting for. That year, I seem to remember, there was a song they kept playing in some of the funkier places with a refrain that went, *Chingado, hechizado* (*Fucked up, spellbound*). That was Jim: fucked up and spellbound. Mexico's spell had bound him and now he was looking his demons right in the face. Let's get out of here, I said. I also asked him if he was high, or feeling ill. He shook his head. The fire-eater was staring at us. Then, with his cheeks puffed out like Aeolus, the god of the winds, he began to approach us. In a fraction of a second I realized that it wasn't a gust of wind we'd be getting. Let's go, I said, and yanked Jim away from the fatal edge of that sidewalk. We took ourselves off down the street toward Reforma, and after a while we went our separate ways. Jim didn't say a word in all that time. I never saw him again.

THE INSUFFERABLE GAUCHO

for Rodrigo Fresán

In the opinion of those who knew him well, Manuel Pereda had two outstanding virtues: he was a caring and affectionate father, and an irreproachable lawyer with a record of honesty, in a time and place that were hardly conducive to such rectitude. As a result of the first virtue, his son and daughter, Bebe and Cuca, whose childhood and adolescent years had been happy, later accused him of having sheltered them from the hard realities of life, focusing their attack particularly on his handling of practical matters. Of his work as a lawyer, there is little to be said. He prospered and made more friends than enemies, which was no mean feat, and when he had the choice between becoming a judge or a candidate for a political party, he chose the bench without hesitation, although it obviously meant giving up the opportunities for greater financial gain that would have been open to him in politics.

After three years, however, disappointed by his judicial career, he gave up public life and spent some time, perhaps even years, reading and traveling. Naturally there was also a Mrs. Pereda, née Hirschman, with whom the lawyer was, so they say, madly in love. There are photos from the time to prove it: in one of them, Pereda, in a black suit, is dancing a tango with a blonde, almost platinum blonde, woman, who is looking at the camera and smiling, while the lawyer's eyes remain fixed on her, like the eyes of a sleepwalker or a sheep. Unfortunately, Mrs. Pereda died suddenly, when Cuca was five and Bebe was seven. The young widower never remarried, although there were various women in his social circle with whom he was known to maintain friendly (though never intimate) relations, and who had, moreover, all the qualities required to become the new Mrs. Pereda.

When the lawyer's two or three close friends asked him why he remained single, his response was always that he didn't want to impose the unbearable burden (as he put it) of a stepmother on his offspring. In Pereda's opinion, most of Argentina's recent problems could be traced back to the figure of the stepmother. As a nation, we never had a mother, he would say, or she was never there, or she left us on the doorstep of the orphanage. But we've had plenty of stepmothers, of all sorts, starting with the great Peronist stepmother. And he would conclude: In Latin America, when it comes to stepmothers, we're the experts.

In spite of everything, his life was happy. It's hard not to be happy, he used to say, in Buenos Aires, which is a perfect blend of Paris and Berlin, although if you look closely it's more like a perfect blend of Lyon and Prague. Every day he got up at the same time as his children, had breakfast with them, and dropped them off at school. He spent the rest of the morning reading at least two newspapers; and, after a snack at eleven (consisting basically of cold cuts and sausage on buttered French bread and two or three little glasses of Argentine or Chilean wine, except on special occasions, when the wine was, naturally, French), he took a siesta until one. His lunch, which he ate on his own in an enormous, empty dining room while reading a book under the absent-minded gaze of the elderly maid, and watched by the black-and-white eyes of his deceased wife, looking out from photographs in ornate silver frames, was light: soup, a small portion of fish and mashed potato, some of which he would leave to go cold. In the afternoon, he helped his children with their homework, or sat through Cuca's piano lessons in silence, or Bebe's English and French classes, given by two teachers with Italian surnames who came to the house. Sometimes, when Cuca had learned to play a piece right through, the maid and the cook would come to listen, and the lawyer, filled with pride, would hear them murmur words of praise, which struck him at first as excessive, but then, on reflection, seemed perfectly apt. After saying good night to his children and reminding his domestic staff for the umpteenth time not to open the door to anyone, he would go to his favorite café, on Corrientes, where he would stay until one at the very latest, listening to his friends or friends of theirs discussing issues that he would have found supremely boring, he suspected, had he known anything about them, after which he would go home, where everyone, by that time, was asleep.

Eventually the children grew up. First Cuca got married and went to live in Rio de Janeiro; then Bebe started writing and indeed became a highly successful writer, which was a source of great pride for Pereda, who read each and every page his son published. Bebe went on living at home for a few more years (where else could he have had it so good?), after which, like his sister, he flew the coop.

At first the lawyer tried to resign himself to solitude. He had an affair with a widow, went on a long trip through France and Italy, met a girl called Rebeca, and finally contented himself with organizing his huge, chaotic library. When Bebe came back from the United States, where he had spent a year teaching at a university, Pereda had aged prematurely. Bebe was worried and tried to spend as much time as he could with his father, so sometimes they went to the movies or the theater, where the lawyer would usually fall into a deep sleep, and sometimes Bebe dragged him along (though he only had to drag him at first) to the literary gatherings held in a café called El Lapiz Negro, where authors basking in the glory of some municipal prize held forth at length about the nation's destiny. Pereda, who never opened his mouth at those gatherings, began to take an interest in what his son's colleagues had to say. When they talked about literature, he was completely bored. In his opinion, the best Argentine writers were Borges and his son; any further commentary on that subject was superfluous. But when they talked about national and international politics, the lawyer's body grew tense, as if under the effect of an electric current. From then on, his daily habits changed. He began to get up early and look through the old books in his library, searching for something, though he couldn't have said what. He spent his mornings reading. He decided to give up wine and heavy meals, because he realized they were dulling his intellect. His personal hygiene also underwent a change. He no longer spruced himself up when he was going out. He soon stopped taking a daily shower. One day he went to read the paper in a park without putting on a tie. His old friends barely recognized this new Pereda as the lawyer they had known, who had been irreproachable in every respect. One day he woke up feeling more agitated than usual. He had lunch with a retired judge and a retired journalist, and laughed all the way through the meal. Afterward, while they were drinking cognac, the judge asked him what he found so funny. Buenos Aires is sinking, Pereda replied. The ex-journalist thought that the lawyer had gone crazy and recommended some time by the seaside: the beach, that invigorating air. The judge, less given to speculation, simply thought that Pereda had gone off on a tangent.

A few days later, however, the Argentine economy collapsed. Accounts in American dollars were frozen, and those who hadn't moved their capital (or their savings) offshore suddenly discovered that they had nothing left, except perhaps a few bonds and bank bills—just looking at them was enough to give you goose bumps—vague promises inspired in equal parts by some forgotten tango and the words of the national anthem. I told you so, said the lawyer to anyone who would listen. Then, accompanied by his cook and maid, he stood in long lines, like many other inhabitants of Buenos Aires, and entered into long conversations with strangers (who struck him as utterly charming) in streets thronged with people swindled by the government or the banks, or some other culprit.

When the president resigned, Pereda was there among the protestors as they banged their pots and pans. It wasn't the only demonstration. Sometimes it seemed that the elderly had taken control of the streets, old people of all social classes, and he liked that, although he didn't know why; it seemed like a sign that something was changing, that something was moving in the darkness, although he was also happy to join in the wildcat strikes and blockades that soon degenerated into brawling. In the space of a few days, Argentina had three different presidents. It didn't occur to anyone to start a revolution, or mount a military coup. That was when Pereda decided to go back to the country.

Before leaving, he explained his plan to the maid and the cook. Buenos Aires is falling apart; I'm going to the ranch, he said. They talked for hours, sitting at the kitchen table. The cook had been to the ranch as often as Pereda, who in the past had always said that the country was no place for a man like him, a cultivated family man, who wanted to make sure that his children got a good education. His mental images of the ranch had blurred and faded, leaving only a house with a hole in the middle, an enormous, threatening tree, and a barn whose dim interior flickered with shadows that might have been rats. Nevertheless, that night, as he drank tea in the kitchen, he told his employees that he had hardly any money left for their wages (it was all frozen in the bank—in other words, as good as lost), and the only solution he could think of was to take them to the country, where at least they wouldn't be short of food, or so he liked to think.

The maid and the cook listened to him compassionately. At one point the lawyer burst into tears. Trying to console him, they told him not to worry about the money; they were prepared to go on working even if he couldn't pay them. The lawyer definitively rejected any such arrangement. I'm too old to become a pimp, he said with an apologetic smile. The next morning, he packed a suitcase and took a taxi to the station. The women waved goodbye from the sidewalk.

The long, monotonous train trip gave him ample time for reflection. At first, the carriage was full. He observed that there were basically two topics of conversation: the country's state of bankruptcy and how the Argentine team was shaping up for the World Cup in Korea and Japan. The press of passengers reminded him of the trains departing from Moscow in the film *Doctor Zhivago*, which he had seen some time before, except that in the Russian carriages as filmed by that English director, the talk was not about ice hockey or skiing. What hope have we got, he thought, although he had to agree that on paper the Argentine selection looked unbeatable. When night fell, the conversations petered out, and the lawyer thought of his children, Cuca and Bebe, both of them abroad; he was also surprised to find himself remembering a number of women with whom he had been intimately acquainted; quietly they emerged from oblivion, their skin covered with perspiration, infusing his restless spirit with a kind of serenity, although it wasn't altogether serene, perhaps not exactly a sense of adventure, but something like that.

Then the train began to advance across the pampas, and the lawyer leaned his head against the cold glass of the window and fell asleep.

When he woke, the carriage was half empty and there was a man who looked part Indian sitting beside him, reading a Batman comic. Where are we? asked Pereda. In Coronel Gutiérrez, said the man. Ah, that's all right, thought the lawyer, I'm going to Capitán Jourdan. Then he got up, stretched his legs, and sat down again. Out on the dry plain he saw a rabbit that seemed to be racing the train. There were five other rabbits running behind it. The first rabbit, running just outside the window, had wide-open eyes, as if the race against the train required a superhuman effort (super-leporine, actually, thought the lawyer). The rabbits in pursuit, on the other hand, seemed to be running in tandem, like cyclists in the Tour de France. With a couple of big leaps, the rabbit bringing up the rear relieved the front-runner, who dropped back to last position, while the third rabbit moved up to second place, and the fourth moved up to third; and all the while the group was closing in on the solitary rabbit running beside the lawyer's window. Rabbits, he thought, how wonderful! On the plains there was nothing else to be seen: a vast, boundless expanse of scanty grass under massive, low clouds, and no indication that a town might be near. Are you going to Capitán Jourdan? Pereda asked the Batman reader, who seemed to be examining every panel with extreme care, scrutinizing every detail, as if he were visiting a portable museum. No, he replied, I'm getting off at El Apeadero. Pereda tried to remember a station of that name but couldn't. And what's that, a station or a factory? The guy with the Indian look stared back at him fixedly: A station, he replied. He seems annoyed, thought Pereda. It wasn't the sort of question he would normally have asked, given his habitual discretion. The pampas had made him inquire in that frank, manly, and down-to-earth way, he thought.

When he rested his forehead against the window again, he saw that the rabbits in pursuit had caught up with the lone racing rabbit, and were attacking it ferociously, tearing at its body with their claws and teeth, those long rodents' teeth, thought Pereda with a horrified frisson. He looked back and saw a bundle of tawny fur thrashing about beside the rails.

The only passengers who got off at the station in Capitán Jourdan were Pereda and a woman with two children. The platform was half wood, half cement, and in spite of his best efforts Pereda couldn't find a railway employee anywhere. The woman and the children set off walking on a cart track, and although they were clearly moving away and their figures were visibly shrinking, it took more than three quarters of an hour, according to the lawyer's reckoning, for them to disappear over the horizon. Is the earth round? Pereda wondered. Of course it is, he told himself, as he settled down for a lengthy wait on an old wooden bench against the wall of the station offices. Inevitably, he remembered Borges's story "The South," and when he thought of the store mentioned in the final paragraphs, tears brimmed in his eyes. Then he remembered the plot of Bebe's last novel, and imagined his son writing on a computer, in an austere office at a Midwestern university. When Bebe comes back and finds out I've gone to the ranch . . . , he thought in enthusiastic anticipation. The glare and the warm breeze blowing off the plain made him drowsy; he fell asleep. A hand shook him awake. A man as old as he was, wearing a worn-out railway uniform, asked him what he was doing there. Pereda said he was the owner of the Alamo Negro ranch. The man stood there looking at him for a while, then said: The judge. That's right, replied Pereda, there was a time when I was a judge. Don't you remember me, Mister Judge? Pereda scrutinized the man: he needed a new uniform and a haircut, urgently. Pereda shook his head. I'm Severo Infante, said the man. We used to play together when we were kids. But, *che*, that's ages ago—how could I remember, Pereda retorted, and the sound of his voice, not to mention the words he had used, sounded odd, as if the air of Capitán Jourdan had invigorated his vocal chords or his throat.

Of course, you're right, Mister Judge, said Severo Infante, but I feel like celebrating anyway. Bouncing like a kangaroo, the station employee disappeared into the ticket office, then came out with a bottle and a glass. Your health, he said, handing Pereda the glass, which he half filled with a clear liquid that seemed to be pure alcohol. Pereda took a sip—it tasted of scorched earth and stones—and left the glass on the bench. He said he had given up drinking. Then he got up and asked the way to his ranch. They went out the back door. Capitán Jourdan is over there, said Severo, just beyond the dry pond. Alamo Negro is the other way, a bit further, but you can't get lost in the daylight. You look after yourself, said Pereda, and set off in the direction of his ranch.

The main house was almost in ruins. That night it was cold, and Pereda tried to gather some sticks and light a campfire, but he couldn't find anything to burn, and in the end he wrapped himself up in his overcoat, rested his head on his suitcase, and told himself, as he fell asleep, that tomorrow would be another day. He woke with the first light of dawn. There was still water in the well, although the bucket had disappeared and the rope was rotten. I need to buy a rope and a bucket, he thought. For breakfast he ate what was left of a packet of peanuts he had bought on the train. He inspected the multitudinous low-ceilinged rooms of the ranch house. Then he set off for Capitán Jourdan, and was surprised to see rabbits but no cattle on the way. He observed them uneasily.

Occasionally they would hop toward him, but he only had to wave his arms to make them disappear. Although he had never been particularly keen on guns, he would have been glad of one then. Apart from that, the walk was pleasant: the air was fresh, the sky was clear; it was neither hot nor cold. From time to time he spotted a tree all alone out on the plain, and the vision struck him as poetic, as if the tree and the austere scenery of the deserted countryside had been arranged just for him, and had been awaiting his arrival with an imperturbable patience.

None of the roads in Capitán Jourdan were paved and the housefronts were thickly coated with dust. As he entered the town, he saw a man asleep beside some flowerpots containing plastic flowers. My god, it's so shabby! he thought. The main square was broad, and the town hall, built of brick, gave the collection of squat, derelict buildings a vague air of civilization. He asked a gardener who was sitting in the square smoking a cigarette where he could find a hardware store. The gardener looked at him curiously, then accompanied him to the door of the only hardware store in town. The owner, an Indian, sold him all the rope he had in stock: forty yards of braided hemp, which Pereda examined at length, as if looking for loose threads. Put it on my account, he said when he had decided what to buy. The Indian looked at him nonplussed. Whose account? he asked. Manuel Pereda's, said Pereda, as he piled up his new possessions in a corner of the store. Then he asked the Indian where he could buy a horse. There are no horses left here, he said, only rabbits. Pereda thought it was a joke and responded with a quick, dry laugh. The gardener, who was looking in from the threshold, said there might be a strawberry roan to be had at Don Dulce's ranch. Pereda asked him how he could get there, and the gardener walked a couple of blocks with him, to a vacant lot full of rubble. Beyond lay open country.

The ranch was called Mi Paraíso and it didn't seem to be as run-down as Alamo Negro. A few chickens were pecking around in the yard. The door to the shed had been pulled off its hinges and someone had propped it against a wall nearby. Some Indian-looking kids were playing with bolas. A woman came out of the main house and said good afternoon. Pereda asked her for a glass of water. Between mouthfuls he asked if there was a horse for sale. You'll have to wait for the boss, said the woman, and went back into the house. Pereda sat down beside the well and kept himself busy brushing away the flies that were buzzing around everywhere, as if the yard were used for pickling meat, thought Pereda, although the only pickles he knew were the ones he used to buy many years ago at a store that imported them directly from England. After an hour, he heard the sound of a jeep and stood up.

Don Dulce was a little pink-faced guy, with blue eyes, wearing a short-sleeved shirt, even though, by the time he arrived, it was starting to get cold. From the jeep emerged an even shorter guy: a gaucho attired in baggy bombachas and a diaper-like *chiripá*, who threw Pereda a sidelong glance and started carrying rabbit skins into the shed. Pereda introduced himself. He said he was the owner of Alamo Negro and that he was planning to do some work on the ranch and needed to buy a horse. Don Dulce invited him to dinner. Around the table sat the host, the woman who had appeared earlier, the children, the gaucho, and Pereda. There was a fire in the hearth, not to heat the room but for grilling meat. The bread was hard and unleavened, the way the Jews make it, thought Pereda, remembering his Jewish wife with a twinge of nostalgia. But no one at Mi Paraíso seemed to be Jewish. Don Dulce spoke like a local, although Pereda did notice a few expressions that were typical of the Buenos Aires loudmouth, as if his host had grown up in Villa Luro and hadn't been living on the pampas all that long.

When it came to buying the horse, everything went smoothly. Choosing was not a problem, because there was only one horse for sale. When Pereda said he might need a month to pay, Don Dulce didn't object, although the gaucho, who hadn't said a word all through the meal, stared at the newcomer warily. They saddled the horse, showed the guest his way home, and said goodbye.

How long has it been since I rode a horse? Pereda wondered. For a few seconds he worried that his bones, accustomed to the comfort of Buenos Aires and its armchairs, might break under the strain. The night was dark as pitch or coal. Stupid expressions, thought Pereda. European nights might be pitch-dark or coal-black, but not American nights, which are dark like a void, where there's nothing to hold on to, no shelter from the elements, just empty, storm-whipped space, above and below. May the rain fall soft on you, he heard Don Dulce shout. God willing, he replied from the darkness.

On the way back to his ranch, he dozed off a couple of times. The first time he saw armchairs raining down over a city, which he eventually recognized as Buenos Aires. Suddenly the armchairs burst into flames, lighting up the city sky as they burned. The other time he saw himself on horseback, with his father, riding away from Alamo Negro. His father seemed to be sad. When will we come back? asked the young Pereda. Never again, Manuelito, said his father. He woke up from this second nap in one of the streets of Capitán Jourdan. He saw a corner store that was open. He heard voices, and someone strumming a guitar, tuning it but never settling on a particular song to play, just as he had read in Borges. For a moment he thought that his destiny, his screwed-up American destiny, would be to meet his death like Dahlman in "The South," and it seemed wrong, partly because he now had debts to repay, and partly because he wasn't ready to die, although Pereda was aware that no one is ever ready for death. Seized by a sudden inspiration, he entered the store on horseback. Inside he found an old gaucho strumming the guitar, the barman, and three younger guys sitting at a table, who started when they saw the horse come in. Pereda was inwardly satisfied by the thought that the scene was like something from a story by di Benedetto. Nevertheless, he set his face and approached the zinc-topped bar. He ordered a glass of eau-de-vie, which he drank with one hand, while in the other he held his riding crop discreetly out of view, since he hadn't yet acquired the traditional sheath knife. He asked the barman to put the drink on his account, and on his way out, as he passed the young gauchos, he told them to move aside because he was going to spit. It was meant as a reaffirmation of authority, but before the gauchos could grasp what was happening, the virulent gob of phlegm had flown from his lips; they barely had time to jump. May the rain fall soft on you, he said, before disappearing into the darkness of Capitán Jourdan.

From then on, Pereda went into town each day on his

horse, which he named José Bianco. He often went to buy tools with which to repair the ranch house, but he also passed the time of day chatting with the gardener, or with the keepers of the general store and the hardware store, whose livelihoods he diminished day by day, as he added to the accounts he had with each of them. Other gauchos and storekeepers soon joined in these conversations, and sometimes even children came to hear the stories Pereda told. The stories, of course, portrayed the teller in a favorable light, although they weren't exactly cheerful. For example he told them how he had once owned a horse very like José Bianco, which had been killed in a confrontation with the police. Luckily I was a judge, he said, and when the police come up against a judge or an ex-judge, they usually back off.

Police work's about order, he said, while judges defend justice. Do you see the difference, boys? The gauchos would usually nod, although not all of them were sure just what he was talking about.

Sometimes he went to the station, where his friend Severo would reminisce at length about their childhood pranks. Although Pereda was privately convinced that he couldn't have been as silly as he came across in those stories, he let Severo talk until he was tired or fell asleep, then walked out onto the platform to wait for the train and the letter it should have been bringing.

Finally the letter arrived. In it, his cook explained that life was hard in Buenos Aires, but that he shouldn't worry, because both she and the maid were going to the house every two days, and it was in perfect order. With the crisis, some apartments in the neighborhood suddenly seemed to have given way to entropy, but his was as clean, as stately, and as comfortable as ever, perhaps even more so, since the usual wear and tear had slowed down to a standstill. Then she went on to relate various pieces of news about the neighbors, gossip tinged with fatalism, since they all felt cheated and no one could see a light at the end of the tunnel. The cook said it was all down to the Peronists, that pack of thieves, while the maid was more sweeping: she blamed all the politicians, and the Argentine people in general; they'd been as docile as sheep, and now they were getting what they deserved. As to sending him money, both of them were looking into it, she assured him; the problem was, they still hadn't figured out how to make sure it wouldn't be filched by some racketeer on the way.

In the evening, as he was returning to Alamo Negro at a gallop, the lawyer could sometimes see a far-off village in ruins that didn't seem to have been there before. Sometimes a slender column of smoke rose from the village and dissipated in the vast sky over the plains. Occasionally he encountered the vehicle in which Don Dulce and his gaucho got around. They would stop to talk and smoke for a while, Don Dulce and the gaucho sitting in their jeep, the lawyer still mounted on José Bianco. Don Dulce was out after rabbits. Pereda once asked him how he hunted them, and Don Dulce told his gaucho to show the lawyer one of the traps, which was half-way between a bird cage and a rat trap. In any case, Pereda never saw a single rabbit in the jeep, only the skins, because the gaucho skinned them on the spot, beside the traps. After those chats, Pereda always felt that Don Dulce was somehow debasing the nation. Rabbit hunting! What sort of job is that for a gaucho? he asked himself. Then he would give his horse an affectionate pat, Come on, *che*, José Bianco, let's go, he'd say, and head back to the ranch.

One day the cook turned up. She had brought money for him. She rode behind him on José Bianco halfway from the station to the ranch, then they walked the rest of the way, in silence, contemplating the plains. By this stage the ranch house was more comfortable than it had been when Pereda arrived; they ate rabbit stew, and then, by the light of an oil lamp, the cook handed over the money she had brought, and explained where it had come from, which objects from the house she had been forced to sell off at a fraction of their value. Pereda didn't even bother to count the bills. The next morning, when he woke up, he saw that the cook had worked all night cleaning up some of the rooms. He reproached her gently. Don Manuel, she said, it's like a pigsty here.

Two days later, in spite of the lawyer's entreaties, she took the train back to Buenos Aires. When I'm away from Buenos Aires I feel like another person, she explained to him as they waited on the platform, just the two of them. And I'm too old to become someone else. Women, they're all the same, thought Pereda. Everything is changing, the cook explained to him. The city was full of beggars, and respectable people were organizing neighborhood soup kitchens just to have something to put in their stomachs. There must have been ten different kinds of currency, not counting the official money. No one was bored. People were desperate, but not bored. As she spoke, Pereda was watching the rabbits that had appeared on the other side of the tracks. The rabbits looked at them, then bounded away across the plain. Sometimes it's as if the country around here was crawling with lice or fleas, thought the lawyer. With the money the cook had brought, he paid his debts and hired a pair of gauchos to repair the roof of the ranch house, which was falling in. The problem was that he knew next to nothing about carpentry, and the gauchos knew even less.

One was called José and must have been around seventy. He didn't have a horse. The other was called Campodónico and was probably younger, though maybe not. Both wore the traditional baggy bombachas, but their headgear consisted of caps they had made themselves from rabbit skins. Neither had a family, so after a while they both came to live at Alamo Negro. At night, by the light of a fire out in the open, Pereda whiled away the time recounting adventures that had taken place exclusively in his imagination. He spoke to them of Argentina, Buenos Aires, and the pampas, and he asked them which one of the three they would choose. Argentina's like a novel, he said, a lie, or make-believe at best. Buenos Aires is full of crooks and loudmouths, a hellish place, with nothing to recommend it except the women, and some of the writers, but only a few. Ah, but the pampas—the pampas are eternal. A limitless cemetery, that's what they're like. Can you imagine that, boys, a limitless cemetery? The gauchos smiled and confessed that it was pretty hard to imagine something like that, since cemeteries are for humans, and although the number of humans is big, there's a limit to it. Ah, but the cemetery I'm talking about, said Pereda, is an exact copy of eternity.

With the money he had left, he went to Coronel Gutiérrez and bought himself a mare and a colt. The mare would let itself be ridden, but the colt was not much use for anything and had to be treated with extreme caution. Sometimes, in the evening, when he was sick of working or sitting around, Pereda went into Capitán Jourdan with his gauchos. He rode José Bianco; the gauchos rode the mare. When he entered the store a respectful hush would fall over the clients, some playing cards, others playing draughts. When the mayor, who was prone to depression, turned up, there would always be four brave volunteers for a game of Monopoly that lasted until dawn. The habit of playing games (not to speak of Monopoly) seemed ill-bred and dishonorable to Pereda. A store is a place where people converse or listen in silence to the conversations of others, he thought. A store is like an empty classroom. A store is a smoky church.

Some nights, especially when gauchos from out of town or some disoriented traveling salesman turned up, Pereda felt a powerful desire to start a fight. Nothing serious, just a scrap, but with real knives, not chalked sticks. Other nights he would fall asleep between his two gauchos and dream that his wife was leading their children by the hand and scolding him for the way he had let himself lapse into brutishness. And what about the rest of the country? replied the lawyer. But that's no excuse, *che*, rejoined Mrs. Pereda, née Hirschman. At which point the lawyer was obliged to agree, with tears welling up in his eyes.

In general, however, his dreams were peaceful, and when he woke up in the morning he was in good spirits and keen to start work. Although, to tell the truth, not a lot of work was done at Alamo Negro. The repairing of the ranch house roof was a disaster. In order to start a kitchen garden, the lawyer and Campodónico bought seeds in Coronel Gutiérrez, but the earth, it seemed, would accept no foreign seed. For a time, the lawyer tried to get the colt, which he called "my stud horse," to cover the mare. If the mare had a filly, all the better. That way, he imagined, he could soon build up a breeding stock that would lead the recovery; but the colt didn't seem to be interested in covering the mare, and although he searched for miles around, Pereda couldn't find a sire, since the gauchos had sold their horses to the slaughterhouse, and now got around on foot, or on bicycles, or hitched rides on the endless dirt tracks of the pampas.

We have fallen, we're down, Pereda would say to his audience, but we can still pick ourselves up and go to our deaths like men. He too had to set rabbit traps to survive. In the evenings, when he left the house with his men, he would often let José and Campodónico empty the traps, along with a new recruit known as the Old Guy, while he set off alone for the ruined village. There he found some young people, younger than his gauchos, but so nervous and disinclined to converse that it wasn't even worth inviting them for a meal. The wire fences were still standing in some places. Occasionally he would go to the railway line and stay there a long time, without dismounting, he and José Bianco both chewing grass stalks, waiting for the train to pass. And often it didn't, as if that part of Argentina had been erased from memory as well as from the map.

One afternoon, as he was vainly attempting to get his colt to mount the mare, he saw a car driving over the plain, coming directly toward Alamo Negro. The car pulled up in the yard and four men got out. At first he didn't recognize his son. Nor did Bebe realize that the old guy in bombachas with a beard, long tangled hair, and a bare chest tanned by the sun was his father. Son of my soul, said Pereda, hugging him, blood of my blood, vindication of my days, and he could have gone on like that if Bebe hadn't stopped him to introduce his friends, two writers from Buenos Aires and the publisher Ibarrola, who loved books and nature, and had financed the trip. In honor of his son's guests, that night the lawyer had a big bonfire built in the yard and sent for the foremost of Capitán Jourdan's guitar-strumming gauchos, warning him beforehand that he was to do strictly that: strum, without playing any song in particular, in accordance with the country way.

Campodónico and José were dispatched to fetch ten liters of wine and a liter of eau-de-vie, which they brought back from Capitán Jourdan in the mayor's van. A good supply of rabbits was laid in, and one was roasted for each person present, although the meat didn't seem to find much favor with the visitors from the city. That night there were more than thirty people gathered around the fire, besides Pereda's gauchos and his guests from Buenos Aires. Before the party began, Pereda announced that he didn't want any fighting or unruly behavior, which was quite unnecessary, since the locals were peace-loving people who had to steel themselves to kill rabbits. All the same, the lawyer considered setting aside one of the multitudinous rooms so that people could lay down their knives, large and small, before taking part in the festivities, but on reflection he decided that such a measure really would be a little excessive.

By three in the morning the elders had set off back to Capitán Jourdan, and there were just a few young men left at the ranch, wondering what to do, since the food and drink had run out, and the guys from the city had already turned in. The next morning Bebe tried to convince his father to return to Buenos Aires with him. Things are gradually settling down, he said; personally he was doing all right. He gave his father a book, one of the many gifts he had brought, and told him that it had been published in Spain. Now I'm known throughout Latin America, he explained. But the lawyer had no idea what his son was talking about. He asked if he was married yet, and when Bebe said no, suggested he find himself an Indian woman and come to live at Alamo Negro.

An Indian woman, Bebe repeated in a tone of voice that struck the lawyer as wistful.

Among the gifts his son had brought was a Beretta 92 pistol with two clips and a box of ammunition. The lawyer looked at the pistol in amazement. Do you honestly think I'm going to need it? he asked. You never know. You're really on your own here, said Bebe. Later that morning they saddled up the mare for Ibarrola, who wanted to take a look at the countryside; Pereda accompanied him on José Bianco. For two hours, the publisher held forth in praise of the idyllic, unspoiled life, as he saw it, enjoyed by the inhabitants of Capitán Jourdan. When he spotted the first of the ruined houses, he broke into a gallop, but it was much further away than he had thought, and before he got there, a rabbit leaped up and bit him on the neck. The publisher's cry vanished at once into the vast open space.

From where he was, all Pereda saw was a dark shape springing from the ground, tracing an arc toward the publisher's head, and then disappearing. Dumb-ass Basque, he thought. He spurred José Bianco, and, approaching Ibarrola, saw that he was holding his neck with one hand and covering his face with the other. Without saying a word, Pereda removed the hand from Ibarrola's neck. There was a bleeding scratch under his ear. Pereda asked him if he had a handkerchief. The publisher replied in the affirmative, and only then did Pereda realize that he was crying. Put the handkerchief on the wound, he said. Then he took the mare's reins and they made their way to the ruined house. There was no one there; they didn't dismount. As they returned to the ranch, the handkerchief that Ibarrola was holding against the wound gradually turned red. They said nothing. When they got back, Pereda ordered his gauchos to strip the publisher to the waist, and they flung him onto a table in the yard. Pereda washed the wound, which he proceeded to cauterize with a knife heated until the blade was red-hot, then made a dressing with another handkerchief, held in place with a makeshift bandage: one of his old shirts, which he soaked in eau-de-vie, what little was left, more as a ritual than a sanitary measure, but it couldn't do any harm.

When Bebe and the two writers came back from a walk around Capitán Jourdan, they found Ibarrola still unconscious on the table, and Pereda sitting beside him in a chair, observing him intently like a medical student. Behind Pereda, equally absorbed by the sight of the wounded man, stood the ranch's three gauchos.

The sun was beating down mercilessly in the yard. Son of a bitch! shouted one of Bebe's friends, your dad's gone and killed our publisher. But the publisher wasn't dead, and made a full recovery, except for the scar, which he would later display with pride, explaining that it had been caused by the bite of a jumping snake and the subsequent cauterization; he even said he felt better than ever, although he did return to Buenos Aires that night with the writers.

From then on, there were often visitors from the city. Sometimes Bebe came on his own, with his riding clothes and his notebooks, in which he wrote vaguely melancholic stories with vaguely crime-related plots. Sometimes he would come with Buenos Aires luminaries, usually writers, but quite often a painter, which pleased Pereda, since painters, for some reason, seemed to know much more about carpentry and bricklaying than the bunch of gauchos who hung around Alamo Negro all day like a bad smell.

On one occasion Bebe came with a psychiatrist. The psychiatrist was blonde and had steely blue eyes and high cheekbones, like an extra from the Ring cycle. The only problem with her, according to Pereda, was that she talked a lot. One morning he invited her to go for a ride. The psychiatrist accepted. He saddled up the mare, mounted José Bianco, and they headed west. As they rode, the psychiatrist talked about her job in a Buenos Aires mental hospital. She told him (and the rabbits that surreptitiously accompanied them for parts of the way) that people were becoming more and more unbalanced—studies had proven it—which led the psychiatrist to conjecture that perhaps mental instability was not so much a disease as a stratum of normality, just below the surface of normality as it was commonly conceived. All this sounded like Chinese to Pereda, but intimidated as he was by the beauty of his son's guest, he refrained from saying so. At midday they stopped for a lunch of rabbit jerky and wine.

The wine and the meat, a dark meat that shone like alabaster when touched by light and seemed to be literally seething with protein, fueled the psychiatrist's poetic streak, and, as Pereda noticed out of the corner of his eye, prompted her to let her hair down.

She began quoting lines from Hernández and Lugones in a well-modulated voice. She wondered aloud where Sarmiento had gone wrong. She ran through lists of books and deeds while the horses trotted imperturbably westward, to places Pereda himself had never reached on previous excursions but was glad to visit in such fine although occasionally tiresome company. At about five in the afternoon, they spotted the shell of a ranch house on the horizon. Enthused, they spurred their mounts in that direction, but at six they were still not there, which led the psychiatrist to remark on how deceptive distances could be. When they finally arrived, five or six malnourished children came out to greet them, and a woman wearing a very wide skirt that bulged voluminously, as if there were some kind of animal under it coiled around her legs. The children kept their eyes fixed on the psychiatrist, who adopted a maternal attitude, though not for long, since she soon noticed, as she later explained to Pereda, a malevolent intention in their gaze, a mischievous plan formulated, so she felt, in a language full of consonants, yelps, and grudges.

Pereda, who was coming to the conclusion that the psychiatrist was not entirely in her right mind, accepted the skirted woman's hospitality, and during the meal, which they ate in a room full of old photographs, he learned that the owners of the ranch had gone off to the city a long time ago (she couldn't say which city), and the laborers, having ceased to receive their monthly pay packet, had gradually drifted away too. The woman also told them about a river and flooding, although Pereda had no idea where the river could be, and no one in Capitán Jourdan had mentioned any kind of flooding. Predictably, they ate rabbit stew, which their hostess had prepared with an expert hand. As they were getting ready to go, Pereda pointed out the way to Alamo Negro, his ranch, in case they ever got tired of living out there. I don't pay much, but at least there's company, he said seriously, as if explaining that death came after life. Then he gathered the children around him and proceeded to dispense advice. When he had finished speaking, he saw that the psychiatrist and the skirted woman had fallen asleep on their chairs. Day was about to break when they left. The light of a full moon shimmered on the plain, and from time to time they saw a rabbit jump, but Pereda paid no attention, and after a long spell of silence he softly began to sing a song in French that his late wife had liked.

The song was about a pier and mist, and faithless lovers (as all lovers are in the end, he thought indulgently), and places that remain steadfastly faithful.

Sometimes, as he walked or rode José Bianco around the dubious boundaries of his ranch, Pereda thought that nothing would ever be the same unless the cattle returned. Cows, he shouted, where are you?

In winter, the skirted woman turned up at Alamo Negro with the children in tow, and things changed. She was known to some people in Capitán Jourdan and they were pleased to see her again. The woman didn't talk much but there could be no doubt that she worked harder than the six gauchos Pereda had on the payroll at the time, loosely speaking, since he often went months without paying them. In any case, some of the gauchos had what could be called an idiosyncratic conception of time. They could adapt to a forty-day month without any major headaches. Or to a four-hundred-and-forty-day year. None of them, in fact, Pereda included, wanted to think about time. By the fireside, some of the gauchos talked about electroshock therapy, while others spoke like professional sports commentators, except that they were commenting on a match played long ago, when they were twenty or thirty and belonged to some gang of hooligans. Sons of bitches, thought Pereda tenderly, with a manly sort of tenderness, of course.

One night, sick of hearing the old guys rambling on about psychiatric hospitals and slums where parents made their children go without milk so they could travel to support their soccer team in some historic match, he asked them about their political opinions. At first the gauchos were reluctant to talk about politics, but when he finally got them to open up, it turned out that, in one way or another, they were all nostalgic for General Perón.

This is where we part company, said Pereda, and pulled out his knife. For a few seconds he thought that the gauchos would do the same and his destiny would be sealed that night, but the old guys recoiled in fear and asked what he was doing, for God's sake. What had they done? What had got into him? The flickering fire threw tiger-like stripes of light across their faces, but, gripping his knife and trembling, Pereda felt that the shame of the nation or the continent had turned them into tame cats. That's why the cattle have been replaced by rabbits, he thought as he turned and walked back to his room.

I'd slaughter the lot of you if you weren't so pathetic, he shouted.

The next morning he was worried that the gauchos might have gone back to Capitán Jourdan, but they were all still there, working in the yard or drinking maté by the fire, as if nothing had happened. A few days later the skirted woman arrived from the ranch out west and Alamo Negro began to change for the better, starting with the food, because the woman knew ten different ways to cook a rabbit, and where to find herbs, and how to start a kitchen garden and grow some fresh vegetables.

One night the woman walked along the veranda and went into Pereda's room. She was wearing only a petticoat; the lawyer made space for her in the bed, and spent the rest of the night looking up at the ceiling and feeling that warm and unfamiliar body against his ribs. Day was breaking by the time he fell asleep, and when he woke up, the woman was gone. Got yourself shacked up, said Bebe when his father informed him. Only technically, the lawyer pointed out. By that stage, with money borrowed here and there, he had been able to enlarge the stables and acquire four cows. When he was bored of an afternoon, he would saddle up José Bianco and take the cows out for a walk. The rabbits, who had never seen a cow in their lives, stared in amazement.

Pereda and the cows looked like they were bound for the ends of the earth, but they had just gone out for a walk.

One morning a doctor and a nurse appeared at Alamo Negro. Having lost their jobs in Buenos Aires, they were working for a Spanish NGO, providing a mobile medical service. The doctor wanted to test the gauchos for hepatitis. When the pair came back a week later, Pereda did his best to put on a feast: rice and rabbit casserole. The doctor said it tasted better than *paella valenciana*, then proceeded to vaccinate all the gauchos free of charge. She gave the cook a bottle of pills and told her to make sure each child took one every morning. Before they left, Pereda asked how his folks were doing health-wise. They're anemic, said the doctor, but no one has Hepatitis B or C. That's a relief, said Pereda. Yes, I guess it is, said the doctor.

As they were getting ready to go, Pereda took a look inside their van. The back was a mess: sleeping bags and boxes full of first-aid supplies: medicines and disinfectants. Where are you going now? he asked. South, said the doctor. Her eyes were red and the lawyer couldn't tell if it was due to lack of sleep or to crying. As the van drove away, raising a cloud of dust, he thought he would miss them.

That night he spoke to the gauchos gathered in the general store. I believe we are losing our memory, he said. And just as well too. For once, the gauchos looked at him as if they had a better grasp of what he was saying than he did himself. Shortly afterward, he received a letter from Bebe summoning him to Buenos Aires: he had to sign some papers so that his house could be sold. Should I take the train, Pereda wondered, or ride? That night he could hardly sleep. He imagined people thronging the sidewalks as he made his entry mounted on José Bianco. Cars stopping, dumbstruck policemen, a newspaper vendor smiling, his compatriots playing soccer in vacant lots with the parsimonious movements of the malnourished. Pereda's entry into Buenos Aires, as he imagined the scene, had the ambiance of Christ's entry into Jerusalem or Brussels as depicted by Ensor. All of us enter Jerusalem sooner or later, he thought as he tossed and turned. Every single one of us. And some never leave. But most do. And then we are seized and crucified. Especially the poor gauchos.

He also imagined a downtown street, the quintessential Buenos Aires street, with all the charms of the capital; he was riding along it on his trusty José Bianco, while from the windows above white flowers began to rain down. Who was throwing the flowers? He couldn't tell, since, like the street itself, the windows of the buildings remained empty. It must be the dead, Pereda supposed drowsily. The dead of Jerusalem and the dead of Buenos Aires.

The next morning he spoke with the skirted woman and the gauchos and told them he would be away for a while. None of them said anything, although that night, at dinner, the woman asked if he was going to Buenos Aires. Pereda nodded. Then take care and may the rain fall soft on you, said the woman.

Two days later, he took the train and went back the way he had come more than three years earlier. When he arrived at Constitución station, a few people stared as if he were wearing fancy dress, but most were not particularly perturbed by an old man attired like a cross between a gaucho and a rabbit trapper. The taxi driver who took him to his apartment inquired where he was from, and when Pereda, lost in his own ruminations, failed to answer, asked if he spoke Spanish. By way of reply, Pereda pulled out his knife and proceeded to trim his nails, which were as long as a wild cat's.

No one answered the door. The keys were under the mat; he went in. The apartment seemed clean, perhaps even too clean—it smelled of mothballs. Feeling exhausted, Pereda trudged to his bedroom and flopped onto the bed without taking off his boots. When he woke up it was dark. He went into the living room without switching on any lights, and called his cook. First he spoke to her husband, who wanted to know who was calling, and didn't sound very convinced when he identified himself. Then the cook came on. I'm in Buenos Aires, Estela, he said. She didn't seem surprised. When asked if she was happy to know that he was back home, she said: There's always something unexpected happening here. Then he tried to call his maid, but an impersonal, female voice informed him that the number he had dialed was not in service. Feeling dispirited and perhaps hungry, he tried to remember the faces of his employees, but the images he could summon were vague: shadows moving in the corridor, a commotion of clean laundry, murmurs and hushed voices.

The amazing thing is that I can remember their phone numbers, thought Pereda, sitting in the dark living room of his apartment. A little later on he went out. Wandering aimlessly, or so he thought, he ended up at the café where Bebe used to meet his artistic and literary friends. From the street he looked into the spacious, well-lit, bustling interior. Bebe and an old man (An old man like me! thought Pereda) were presiding over one of the most animated tables. At another, closer to the window through which Pereda was spying, he noticed a group of writers who looked more like advertising executives. One of them, with an adolescent air, although he was at least fifty and maybe even over sixty, kept putting a white powder up his nose and holding forth about world literature. Suddenly, the eyes of the pseudo-adolescent met Pereda's. For a moment their gazes locked, as if, for each of them, the presence of the other was a gash in the ambient reality. Resolutely and with surprising agility, the writer with the adolescent air sprang to his feet and rushed out into the street. Before Pereda knew what was going on, the writer was upon him.

What are you staring at? he demanded, brushing remnants of white powder from his nose. Pereda looked him up and down. The writer was taller and slimmer and possibly stronger than he was. What are you staring at, you rude old fool? What are you staring at? The pseudo-adolescent's gang was looking on, following the scene as if something similar happened every night.

Pereda realized that he had grasped his knife, and let himself go. He took a step forward and, without anyone noticing that he was armed, planted the point of the blade, though not deeply, in his opponent's groin. Later, he would remember the look of surprise on the writer's face, in which terror was blended with something like reproof, and the words with which he groped for an explanation (Hey, what are you doing, you asshole?), as if there were any way to explain fever and revulsion.

I think you need a napkin, Pereda remarked in a clear strong voice, pointing at his adversary's bloodstained crotch. Mother, said the cokehead, looking down. When he looked up again, he was surrounded by friends and colleagues, but Pereda was gone.

What should I do, the lawyer wondered as he roamed through his beloved city, finding it strange and familiar, marvelous and pathetic. Do I stay in Buenos Aires and become a champion of justice, or go back to the pampas, where I don't belong, and try to do something useful . . . I don't know, something with the rabbits, maybe, or the locals, those poor gauchos who accept me and put up with me and never complain? The shadows of the city declined to provide an answer. Keeping quiet, as usual, Pereda thought reproachfully. But when the day began to dawn, he decided to go back.

POLICE RAT

for Robert Amutio and Chris Andrews

My name is José, though people call me Pepe, and some, usually those who don't know me well, or with whom I'm not on familiar terms, call me Pepe the Cop. Pepe is a benign, well-meaning, genial diminutive, neither scornful nor flattering, and yet the appellation does imply, if I can put it this way, a certain affection, something more than detached respect. Then there's the other name, the alias, the tail or the hump that I lug around cheerfully, without taking offense, partly because it's never or almost never used in my presence. Pepe the Cop: it's like tossing affection and fear, desire and abuse into the same dark bag. Where does the word *cop* come from? It comes from *copper*, he who cops or caps, that is captures, takes hold of, nabs, in other words, he who has the authority to arrest and hold, who doesn't have to answer to anyone, who has *impunity*. And they call me Pepe the Cop because that's exactly what I am; it's a job like any other, but few people are prepared to take it on. If I'd known what I know now when I joined the force, I wouldn't have been prepared to take it on either. What made me join the police force? That's a question I've often asked myself, especially lately, and I can't come up with a convincing answer.

I was probably dimmer than most in my youth. Maybe I was disappointed in love (though I can't actually recall being in love at the time), or maybe it was fate; maybe I realized I was different, and looked for a solitary job, a job that would allow me to spend hour after hour in the most absolute solitude, but would, at the same time, be of some practical use, so I wouldn't be a burden on anyone.

In any case, there was a vacancy for a police officer and I applied and the bosses took a look at me, and in less than half a minute the job was mine. One of them at least, and maybe the others as well, already knew that I was one of Josephine the Singer's nephews, although they were careful not to go spreading it around. My brothers and cousins—the other nephews—were normal in every way, and happy. I was happy too in my way, but it was obvious that I was related to Josephine, that I belonged to her line. Maybe that influenced the bosses' decision to give me the job. Or not—maybe I was just the first to apply. Maybe they thought no one else would, and if they made me wait, I'd change my mind. I really can't say. All I know for sure is that I joined the force and from the very first day I spent my time wandering through the sewers, sometimes the main ones, where the water flows, sometimes the branch sewers, where we are constantly digging tunnels to gain access to new food sources or provide escape routes or link up with labyrinths that seem, at first glance, to serve no purpose, and yet all those byways go to make up the network in which our people circulate and survive.

Sometimes, partly because it was one of my duties and partly because I was bored, I'd leave the main sewers and the branch ones too and go into the dead sewers, conduits frequented only by our explorers and traders, usually on their own, but occasionally accompanied by their spouses and obedient offspring. There was nothing in there, as a rule, just terrifying noises, but sometimes, as I made my way cautiously through that hostile territory, I would come across the body of an explorer or the bodies of a trader and his young children. In the early days, when I was still raw, those discoveries terrified me; I would be so disturbed it was as if I became someone else. What I would do was carry the body out from the dead sewer to the police outpost, which was always deserted, and there I'd try to determine the cause of death as well as I could with the means at my disposal. Then I would go to fetch the coroner, and if he was in the mood, he'd get dressed or change his clothes, grab his bag, and accompany me to the outpost. Once we were there, I'd leave him alone with the corpse or the corpses and go out again. When our police officers discover a body, instead of returning to the scene of the crime, they generally make a vain effort to mix with civilians, working alongside them and participating in their conversations, but I'm different, I don't mind going back to inspect the crime scene and look for details that might have escaped my notice, and retrace the poor victims' steps or sniff my way, cautiously of course, back up the tunnel from which the attack had been launched.

After a few hours I'd return to the outpost and find the coroner's note tacked to the wall. Causes of death: slit throats, loss of blood, broken necks; and there were often lacerations to the paws—our kind never give in without a fight, we struggle to the last. The killer was usually some carnivore that had strayed into the sewers, a snake, sometimes even a blind alligator. There was no point pursuing them; most died of hunger before long anyway.

When I took a break I'd seek out the company of other police officers. I met one who was very old and withered by age and work; he had known my aunt and liked to talk about her. Nobody understood Josephine, he said, but everyone loved her or pretended to, and she was happy—or pretended to be. Those words were Chinese to me, like a lot of what that old officer said. I've never understood music; it's not an art that we practice, except on rare occasions. In fact, we don't practice (and therefore don't understand) any of the arts, really. Every now and then a rat who paints, for example, will appear in our midst, or a rat who writes poems and takes it into his head to recite them. As a general rule, we don't make fun of those individuals. On the contrary, we pity them, because we know that they're condemned to solitude. Why? Well, because creating works of art and contemplating them are activities in which our people as a rule are unable to take part, and the exceptions, the *mavericks*, are very few, so if, for example, a poet or even just a reciter of poetry comes along, it's most unlikely that another poet or reciter will be born in the same generation, which means that the poet may never encounter the only individual capable of appreciating his efforts. Which is not to say that we won't interrupt our daily occupations to listen to the poet or applaud him, or even move that the reciter be granted a pension. On the contrary, we do everything in our power—or rather what little we can—to provide the *maverick* with a simulation of understanding and affection, since we know that, fundamentally, affection is what he or she requires. Any simulation, however, collapses eventually, like a house of cards. We live in a collective, and what the collective depends on is, above all, the daily labor, the ceaseless activity of each of its members, working toward a goal that transcends our individual aspirations but is nevertheless the only guarantee of our existence as individuals.

Of all the artists we have known, or at least of those who remain in our memories like skeletal question marks, the greatest was, without a doubt, my aunt Josephine. Great in the sense that she made exceptional demands on us; incommensurably great in the sense that our community acquiesced or pretended to acquiesce to her whims.

The old police officer liked to talk about her, but his memories, I soon realized, were as flimsy as cigarette paper. Sometimes he said that Josephine was fat and tyrannical, and that dealing with her required enormous patience or an enormous sense of sacrifice, two not unrelated virtues, both quite common among us. Sometimes, however, by contrast, he said that all he had glimpsed of Josephine—he'd have been an adolescent, just starting out in the force—was a shadow, a tremulous shadow, trailing a range of odd squeaking noises, which constituted, at the time, the entirety of her repertoire, yet could, if not transport her listeners, certainly plunge some of those in the front row into a state of extreme sadness. Those rats and mice, of whom we have no record now, are perhaps the only ones to have glimpsed something in my aunt's musical art. But what? They probably didn't know themselves. Something indefinite, a lake of emptiness. Something resembling the desire to eat, perhaps, or the need to fuck, or the longing for sleep that sometimes overtakes us, since those who work without respite must at least sleep from time to time, especially in winter, when the temperature falls, as they say the leaves fall from the trees in the outside world, and our chilled bodies yearn for a warm corner to share with our kind, a burrow full of hot fur and the familiar movements and sounds—such as they are, neither coarse nor gracious—of our everyday nocturnal life, or the life that we call nocturnal for the sake of convenience.

The difficulty of finding warm places to sleep is one of the main disadvantages of being a police officer. We generally sleep alone, in makeshift holes, sometimes in unfamiliar territory, although of course, whenever possible, we try to find an alternative. Sometimes, but not very often, we curl up in holes that we share with other police, all eyes shut, ears and noses on alert. And sometimes we go to the sleeping quarters of those who, for one reason or another, live along the perimeter. As you would expect, they are quite unperturbed by our presence. Sometimes we say good night before falling exhausted into a warm and restorative sleep. Sometimes we simply mumble our names; our hosts know who we are and know they have nothing to fear from us. They treat us well. They don't make a fuss or show any sign of joy, but they don't throw us out of their burrows. Occasionally someone will say, in a voice still thick with sleep, Pepe the Cop, and I will reply, Yes, yes, good night. After a few hours, however, while all the others are still sleeping, I get up and start again, because police work is never done, and our hours of sleep have to be fitted in around the incessant demands of the job. Patrolling the sewers is a task that requires the utmost concentration. Generally we don't see or meet with anyone; we can do the rounds of the main and branch sewers, and go into the disused tunnels originally dug by our people, all without coming across a single living being.

We do, however, glimpse shadows, and hear noises—objects falling into the water, distant squeaking. At the beginning, when you're new to the job, you're hypersensitive to those noises and you live in a state of perpetual fright. As time goes by, however, you grow accustomed to them, and although you try to stay alert, you lose the fear, or build it into the daily routine, which is the same as losing it, in the end. There are even police officers who have slept in the dead sewers. I have never met one personally, but the old guys often tell stories in which an officer, back in the old days, of course, overtaken by fatigue, would curl up and go to sleep in a dead sewer. How seriously should we take those stories? I don't know. No police officer today would dare to do such a thing. The dead sewers are places that have been forgotten for one reason or another. When the tunnel-diggers reach a dead sewer, they block the tunnel. The water in them barely flows at all, so the putrefaction is almost unbearable. It is safe to say that our people only use the dead sewers to flee from one zone to another. The quickest way to get into them is by swimming, but swimming in such places involves greater risks than we are usually prepared to take.

It was in a dead sewer that my investigation began. A group of our pioneers who, over time, had multiplied and settled just beyond the perimeter came and told me that the daughter of one of the older rats had disappeared. While half the group worked, the other half went looking for this girl, who was called Elisa, and who, according to her relatives and friends, was very beautiful and strong, as well as possessing a lively intelligence. I wasn't sure exactly what possessing a lively intelligence meant. I associated it vaguely with cheerfulness, but not curiosity. I was tired that day, and after examining the area in the company of one of the missing girl's relatives, I conjectured that the unfortunate Elisa had been the victim of some predator roaming in the vicinity of the new colony. I looked for traces of the predator. All I found were old tracks, which showed that other creatures had passed that way, before the arrival of our pioneers.

Finally I discovered a trail of fresh blood. I told Elisa's relative to go back to the burrow and I continued on my own. The trail of blood was curious: it kept stopping at the edge of a canal, but then reappearing a few yards further on (and sometimes *many* yards further), always on the same side, not the far side, as one might have expected. Whatever had left that trail clearly wasn't trying to cross the canal, so why had it kept getting into the water? In any case, the trail itself was barely detectable, so the precautions taken by the predator, whatever it was, seemed, at first, to be excessive. After a while I came to a dead sewer.

I got into the water there, and swam toward a bank of accumulated rotting trash, and when I reached it I had to climb up a beach of filth. Beyond the bank, above water level, I could see the thick bars at the top of the sewer's entrance. For a moment I was afraid I might find the predator huddled in some corner, feasting on the body of the hapless Elisa. But I could hear nothing, so I kept going.

A few minutes later, among cardboard boxes and old food cans, I found the girl's body left in one of the few relatively dry parts of the sewer.

Elisa's neck was torn open. Apart from that, I couldn't see any other wound. In one of the cans I found the remains of a baby rat. I examined them: dead for at least a month. I searched the surroundings but couldn't detect the slightest trace of the predator. The baby's corpse was complete. The only wound on poor Elisa's body was the one that had killed her. I began to think that perhaps it hadn't been a predator. Then I put the girl on my back and picked up the baby in my mouth, trying not to damage his skin with my sharp teeth. I retreated from the dead sewer and returned to the pioneers' burrow. Elisa's mother was large and strong, one of those specimens who can face up to a cat, but when she saw the body of her daughter, she burst into long sobs that made her companions blush. I showed them the body of the baby and asked them if they knew anything about him. No one knew anything, no child had been lost. I said that I had to take both bodies to the station. I asked for help. The mother carried Elisa's body. I carried the baby. When we left, the pioneers returned to work, digging tunnels, looking for food.

This time I went to fetch the coroner and stayed with him until he finished examining both bodies. Elisa's mother, asleep beside us, was seized from time to time by dreams, which wrested incomprehensible and incoherent words from her. After three hours the coroner had decided what he was going to tell me; it was what I had been afraid to imagine. The baby had died of hunger; Elisa had died from the wound to her throat. I asked him if that wound could have been inflicted by a snake. I don't think so, said the coroner, unless it's a new kind of snake. I asked him if the wound could have been inflicted by a blind alligator. Impossible, said the coroner. Maybe a weasel, he said. Weasels have been seen in the sewers recently. Scared to death, I said. That's true, replied the coroner. Most of them die of hunger. They get lost, they drown, they're eaten by alligators. We can forget the weasels, said the coroner. Then I asked him if Elisa had struggled with her killer. The coroner looked at the girl's corpse for a long time. No, he concluded. That's what I thought, I said. While we were talking, another police officer appeared. His rounds, as opposed to mine, had been quite uneventful. We woke Elisa's mother. The coroner said goodbye. Is it all over? asked the mother. It's all over, I replied. She thanked us and left. I asked my colleague to help me get rid of Elisa's corpse.

The two of us took it to a canal where the current was strong and threw it in. Why don't you throw out the baby's body too? asked my colleague. I don't know, I said, I want to examine it, maybe we missed something. Then he went back to his beat and I went back to mine. I asked every rat I met the same question: Have you heard anything about a missing baby? I got all sorts of answers, but in general our people look after their young, and what they told me was all secondhand. My rounds took me back to the perimeter. The pioneers were working on a tunnel, all of them, including Elisa's mother, whose bulky, greasy body could barely squeeze through the crack, but her teeth and claws were still the best for digging.

I decided to go back to the dead sewer and try to see what it was that I had missed. I looked for tracks but couldn't find any. Signs of violence. Signs of life. The baby hadn't made its own way into the sewer, that much was obvious. I looked for food scraps, traces of dried shit, a burrow, all in vain.

Suddenly I heard a faint splashing. I hid. After a while I

saw a white snake break the surface of the water. It was thick and must have been a yard long. I saw it dive and resurface a couple of times. Then it emerged cautiously from the water and scaled the bank, making a hissing sound like a leaking gas pipe. For our people, that snake was as lethal as gas. It approached my hiding place. Coming from that direction, it couldn't attack directly, which meant, in principle, that I had time to escape (but once in the water I would be easy prey) or sink my teeth into its neck. It was only when the snake went away without any sign of having seen me that I realized it was blind, a descendant of those pet snakes that humans flush down the toilet when they get tired of them. For a moment I felt sorry for it. And I celebrated my good luck in an indirect way. I imagined the snake's parents or great-great-grandparents descending through the infinite network of sewer pipes; I imagined their bewilderment in the darkness of the sewers, not knowing what to do, resigned to death or suffering, and I imagined the few that survived, adapting themselves to an infernal diet, exercising their power, sleeping and dying in that endless winter.

Fear stimulates the imagination, it seems. When the snake was gone, I resumed my methodical search of the dead sewer. I didn't find anything out of the ordinary. The next day I talked with the coroner again. I asked him to take another look at the baby's corpse. At first he looked at me as if I'd gone insane. Haven't you got rid of it? he asked. No, I said, I want you to check it over one more time. Eventually he promised he would, as long as he didn't have too much work that day. As I did my rounds, waiting for the coroner's final report, I kept looking for a family that had lost a baby in the previous month. Unfortunately, the work we do, especially those who live near the perimeter, keeps us constantly on the move, and by then the mother of the dead baby could well have been digging tunnels or searching for food several miles away. Unsurprisingly, my inquiries didn't yield any promising leads.

When I returned to the station I found a note from the coroner—and another from my commanding officer, asking me why I still hadn't got rid of the baby's corpse. The coroner's note confirmed his earlier conclusion: there were no wounds; the cause of death had been hunger and possibly also exposure to the cold. The little ones are particularly vulnerable to harsh environmental conditions. I thought about it long and hard. The baby must have cried itself hoarse, as any baby would in a situation like that. Surely his cries would have attracted a predator? Why hadn't they? The killer must have snatched the baby, then used back ways to reach the dead sewer. And there, he had left the baby alone and waited for him to die, of natural causes, as it were. Could it have been the baby snatcher who later killed Elisa? Yes, that was the most likely scenario.

Then a question occurred to me, something I hadn't asked the coroner, so I got up and went looking for him. On the way, I saw many rats who seemed carefree or playful or preoccupied with their own problems, scurrying in one direction or the other. Some of them greeted me warmly. Someone said, Look, there goes Pepe the Cop. The only thing I could feel was the sweat beginning to soak all through my fur, as if I'd just crawled out of the stagnant waters of a dead sewer.

I found the coroner sleeping alongside five or six other rats, all of them, to judge from their weariness, doctors or medical students. When I roused him from his sleep he looked at me as if he didn't know who I was. How many days did he take to die? I asked him. José, is that you? asked the coroner. What do you want? How many days does it take a baby to die of hunger? We left the burrow. Why did I ever become a pathologist? said the coroner. Then he thought for a while. It depends on the baby's constitution. Two days or less in some cases, but a plump, well-nourished baby could last five days or more. And without drinking? I asked. A bit less, said the coroner. Then he added: I don't know what you're trying to get at. Did he die of hunger or thirst? I asked. Hunger. Are you sure? As sure as you can be in a case like this, said the coroner.

Back at the station I got to thinking: the baby had been taken a month ago and probably took three or four days to die. He must have been crying all that time. And yet the noise hadn't attracted any predators. I returned to the dead sewer once again. This time I knew what I was looking for and it didn't take me long to find it: a gag. All the time he was dying, the baby had been gagged. No, not *all* the time. Every now and then the killer had taken off the gag and given the baby a drink, or maybe left it on, but soaked the cloth with water. I picked up what was left of the gag and got out of that dead sewer.

The coroner was waiting for me at the station. What did you find there, Pepe? he asked when he saw me. The gag, I said, handing him the scrap of dirty cloth. The coroner examined it for a few seconds, without touching it. Is the baby's body still here? he asked me. Get rid of it, he said, people are starting to talk about the way you're behaving. Talk about or criticize? I asked. It comes to the same thing, said the coroner before he left. I didn't feel up to working, but I pulled myself together and went out. Apart from the usual accidents, which can be relied upon to blight everything we undertake, it was a routine beat like any other. When I returned to the station, after hours of exhausting work, I got rid of the baby's body. For days there were no new developments. There were attacks by predators, accidents, old tunnels collapsed, several of our number were killed by a poison before we could find a way to neutralize it. Our history consists of the various ways we find to elude the traps that open endlessly before us. Routine and mettle. Recovering bodies and recording incidents. Identical, calm days. Until I found the bodies of two young rats, a female and a male.

I had heard they were missing on my rounds of the tunnels. The parents weren't worried; they thought the young couple had probably decided to go and live together in a different burrow. But as I was leaving, not overly preoccupied by the double disappearance, someone who had been friends with them both told me that neither the young Eustaquio nor the young Marisa had ever expressed any such wish. They're just friends, good friends, which is remarkable given Eustaquio's peculiarity. And what kind of peculiarity is that? I asked. He composes and declaims verse, said the friend (so he was obviously unfit for work). And what about Marisa? Not her, said the friend. What do you mean, not her? I asked. She doesn't have any peculiarity like that. To another police officer, these details would have seemed irrelevant. But my instincts were alerted. I asked if there was a dead sewer anywhere near the burrow. They told me that the closest one was a mile away, at a lower level. I set off in that direction.

Along the way I came across an old rat followed by a group of youngsters. The old guy was warning them about weasels. We said hello. He was a teacher leading an excursion. The youngsters weren't ready yet for work, but nearly. I asked them if they'd noticed anything strange in the course of their outing. Everything is strange, shouted the old guy, as we went off in opposite directions, strange is normal, fever is health, poison is food. Then he burst into cheerful laughter, which went on ringing in my ears, even when I turned into another passage.

After a while I came to the dead sewer. Sewers in which the water is stagnant are all pretty much the same, but I can usually tell, with a fair degree of certainty, whether or not I've been in a particular dead sewer before. That one was unfamiliar. I examined the entrance for a while, looking for a dry way in. Then I jumped into the water and swam. As I drew closer I thought I could see waves coming from an island of detritus. Naturally, I was worried about running into a snake, and I swam toward the island as quickly as I could. The ground there was soft; I sunk into a whitish mud up to my knees. The smell was the same as in all the dead sewers, not decomposing matter so much as the inner essence of decomposition. I made my way slowly from island to island. Occasionally I had the impression that something was clutching at my feet, but it was only trash. On the last island I found the bodies. There was only one wound on young Eustaquio's body: his throat was torn open. It was clear that young Marisa, however, had put up a fight. Her skin was covered with bites. I found blood on her teeth and claws, from which it was simple to deduce that the killer had been wounded. I struggled with the bodies one at a time, and finally got them out of the sewer. Then I tried to transport them to the nearest settlement, carrying one for fifty yards, putting it down, going back for the other. At one point, as I was going back for young Marisa's body, I saw a white snake that had come out of the canal and was heading toward her. I froze. The snake wrapped itself twice around her body, then crushed it. When it began to swallow her, I turned and ran to where I'd left Eustaquio. I wanted to scream. But I didn't even let out a whimper.

From that day on, I intensified my investigations. I was no longer satisfied with routine police work: patrolling the perimeter and dealing with problems that anyone with a modicum of common sense could solve. Every day I went out to the furthest burrows. I engaged their inhabitants in the most trivial conversations. I discovered a colony of rat-moles living among us, performing the lowliest tasks. I met an old white mouse, a white mouse who couldn't remember his age. In his youth he had been inoculated with a contagious disease, along with many of his kind, white mice who had been imprisoned and then released into the sewers in the hope of killing us all. Many died, said the white mouse, who could barely move, but the black rats and the white mice interbred, we fucked like crazy (as only those who are close to death can fuck) and in the end not only did the black rats become immune, but a new species also emerged: brown rats, resistant to any infection, any alien virus.

I liked that old white mouse who was born, so he said, in a laboratory on the surface. The light is blinding up there, he said, so bright that the surface dwellers don't even appreciate it. Have you been to the sewer mouths, Pepe? Yes, once or twice, I replied. So you've seen the river that the sewers all flow into, you've seen the reeds, the pale sand? Yes, but always at night, I replied. So you've seen the moonlight shimmering on the river? I didn't really notice the moonlight. What did you notice, then, Pepe? The barking of the dogs, the packs of dogs that live by the river. The moonlight too, I admitted, but I couldn't really enjoy the view. The moon is exquisite, said the white mouse; if someone were to ask me where I'd like to live, I would reply without hesitation: the moon.

Like a moon-dweller I patrolled the sewers and underground drains. After a while I found another victim. As before, the killer had left the body in a dead sewer. I picked it up and carried it to the station. That night I spoke with the coroner again. I pointed out the similarity between the tear in the throat and the other victims' wounds. It could be a coincidence, he said. And whatever's doing this doesn't eat them, I said. The coroner examined the body. Look at the wound, I said. Tell me what kind of teeth rip the skin like that. Any kind, any kind, said the coroner. No, not any kind, look carefully. What do you want me to say? said the coroner. The truth, I said. And what is the truth, in your opinion? I think these wounds were made by a rat, I said. But rats don't kill rats, said the coroner, looking at the body again. This one does, I said. Then I went to work and when I returned to the station I found the coroner and the chief commissioner waiting for me. The commissioner didn't beat around the bush. He asked me where I'd got the crazy idea that a rat had been responsible for the crimes. He wanted to know if I had shared my suspicions with anyone else. He warned me not to. Stop fantasizing, Pepe, he said, and concentrate on doing your job. Real life is complicated enough without inventing unreal things that are bound to throw it out of joint. I was dead tired; I asked him what he meant by *out of joint.* I mean, said the commissioner, looking at the coroner as if to seek his approval and adopting a deep and gentle tone of voice, that in life, especially if it's short, as our lives unfortunately are, we should strive for order, not disorder, and especially not an imaginary disorder. The coroner looked at me gravely and nodded. I nodded too.

But I remained alert. For several days the killer seemed to have disappeared. Every time I went to the perimeter and made contact with a new colony, I asked about the first victim, the baby who had died of hunger. Finally an old explorer told me about a mother who had lost her baby. They thought it had fallen into the canal or been taken by a predator. But since there were many children in that group and only a few adults, they didn't spend a long time looking for the baby. Shortly afterward, they moved to the northern sewers, near a big well, and the explorer lost touch with them. When I had some time to spare, I went looking for that group. I knew they would have multiplied since the baby's disappearance; the children would have grown up, and perhaps they would have forgotten. But if I was lucky enough to find the baby's mother, she would still be able to tell me something. The killer, meanwhile, was on the loose. One night I found a body in the morgue with the killer's signature wound: the throat was torn open, almost neatly. I spoke with the police officer who had found the body. I asked him if he thought it had been a predator. What else could it be? he said. You think it was an accident, do you, Pepe? An accident, I thought. A permanent accident. I asked him where he had found the body.

In a dead sewer down south, he replied. I suggested that he keep an eye on the dead sewers in that sector. Why? he wanted to know. Because you never know what you'll find there. He looked at me as if I were crazy. You're tired, he said, let's get some sleep. We went to the station's sleeping room. The air was warm. Another police rat was snoring in there. Good night, said my colleague. Good night, I said, but I couldn't sleep. I started thinking about the killer's movements, the way he sometimes struck in the north and sometimes in the south. After tossing and turning for a while I got up.

I headed north, stumbling along. On the way I came across some rats who were setting off to work in the dim tunnels; they were confident and resolute. I heard some youngsters saying, Pepe the Cop, Pepe the Cop, then laughing, as if my nickname were the funniest joke in the world. Or maybe they were laughing for some other reason. In any case I didn't stop.

Gradually the tunnels were all deserted. Only now and then did I encounter a pair of rats or hear them going about their business down other tunnels, or glimpse their shadows huddled around something that could have been food, or poison. After a while, the noises stopped and I could hear only the sound of my heart and the dripping that never ceases in our world. When I came to the big well, the reek of death made me tread even more warily. Half consumed by maggots, the carcasses of two average-size dogs lay there, rigid, paws sticking up.

The colony of rats I'd been looking for was also exploiting the canine remains, a little further on. They were living near the sewer mouth, with all the dangers that entails, but also the advantage of extra food, which is never scarce on the frontier. I found them gathered in a small open space. They were big and fat and their coats were glossy. They had the serious expression of those who live in constant danger. When I told them I was a police officer, a suspicious look came into their eyes. When I told them I was looking for a rat who had lost her baby, no one answered, but from their expressions I could tell straightaway that my search, or that part of it at least, was over. Then I described the baby, his age, the dead sewer where I had found him, the way he had died. One of the rats said that the baby was her son. What do you want? asked the others.

Justice, I said. I'm looking for the killer.

The oldest rat, with a scar-covered hide, asked me, puffing like a bellows, if I thought the killer was one of them. It could be, I said. A rat? she asked. It could be. The mother said her baby used to go out alone. But he couldn't have got into a dead sewer alone, I replied. Maybe he was taken by a predator, said a young rat. A predator would have eaten the body. This baby was killed for pleasure, not food.

As I'd expected, they all shook their heads. It's unthinkable, they said. There's no way one of us, however crazy, could be capable of something like that. Still smarting from the police commissioner's words, I judged it wiser not to contradict them. I nudged the mother to an out-of-the-way place and tried to console her, although the truth is that after three months—that was how long it had been—the pain of the loss had considerably diminished. She told me that she had other children, some grown up and hard for her to recognize, and some younger than the one who had died who were already working and foraging successfully on their own. Nevertheless, I tried to get her to remember the day when the baby had disappeared. At first she was confused. She got the days mixed up; she even mixed up her babies. Alarmed by this, I asked her if she had lost more than one, but she reassured me, saying, No, babies do get lost, though usually only for a few hours, and they either come back to the burrow on their own, or are found when a member of the group hears them crying. Your son cried too, I said, slightly annoyed by her self-satisfied expression, but the killer kept him gagged most of the time.

She didn't seem moved, so I went back to the day of the baby's disappearance. We weren't living here, she said, we were in a drain in the interior. A group of explorers was living nearby; they had been the first to settle in the area, and then another group came, a bigger one, and we decided to move; we had no alternative really, apart from wandering around the tunnels. I pointed out that in spite of all this, the children were well nourished. There wasn't a shortage of food, but we had to go and search for it outside. The explorers had dug tunnels that led directly to the upper regions, and no poison or traps could stop us. All the groups went up to the surface twice a day, at least; there were rats who spent whole days up there, wandering through the old half-ruined buildings, using the cavities in the walls to get around, and there were some who never came back.

I asked her if they were outside the day her baby disappeared. We were working in the tunnels, some were sleeping, and there were probably some outside as well, she replied. I asked her if she'd noticed anything strange about anyone in the group. Strange? Abnormal behavior or attitudes; long, unexplained absences. No, she said, as you should know, the way we behave depends on the situation; we try to adapt to it as quickly and as fully as possible. Shortly after the baby's disappearance, in any case, the group set off to find a safer area. I could tell I wouldn't get anything more out of that simple, hardworking rat. I said goodbye to the group and left the drain they were using as their burrow.

But I didn't return to the station that day. Halfway there, when I was sure no one had followed me, I doubled back and went looking for a dead sewer near the drain. After a while I found one. It was small and the stench wasn't overpowering. I examined it thoroughly. The rat I was looking for didn't seem to have used that place. Nor did I find signs of predators. Although there wasn't a dry place anywhere, I decided to stay. In order to make myself a little more comfortable, I gathered what pieces of damp cardboard and plastic I could find and settled myself on them. I imagined the warmth of my fur against the damp materials producing little clouds of steam. The steam began to make me feel drowsy; then it seemed to be forming a dome within which I was invulnerable. I'd almost fallen asleep when I heard voices.

Before long they appeared in the distance: two young male rats, talking animatedly. I recognized one of them straightaway—he was from the group that I had just visited. The other one was completely unfamiliar; maybe he'd been working at the time of my visit, maybe he belonged to another group. The discussion they were having was heated, but without overstepping the bounds of civility. Their arguments were incomprehensible, partly because they were still a way off (though, splashing through the shallow water on their little paws, they were heading straight for my refuge), and partly because they were using words that belonged to another language, a language that rang false, that was alien to me, and instantly revolting: words like pictograms or ciphers, words that crawl on the underside of the word *freedom*, as fire is said to crawl into the tunnels, turning them into ovens.

I would have liked to scurry away discreetly. But my police instincts were telling me that unless I intervened, another murder was about to be committed. I jumped off the pile of cardboard. The two rats froze. Good evening, I said. I asked them if they belonged to the same group. They shook their heads.

You, I said, pointing to the rat I didn't know with my paw, out of here. The young rat seemed to have a reputation to defend; he hesitated. Out of here, I'm a police officer, I said. I'm Pepe the Cop, I shouted. Then he glanced at his friend, turned, and left. Watch out for predators, I said to him before he disappeared behind a mound of trash, there's no one to help you if you get attacked by a predator in the dead sewers.

The other rat didn't even bother to say goodbye to his friend. He stayed there with me, quietly, waiting until we were alone, with his thoughtful little eyes fixed on me, as I guess mine were studying him. I've got you, finally, I said when we were alone. He didn't answer. What's your name? I asked. Hector, he said. Now that he was speaking to me, his voice was no different from thousands I had heard. Why did you kill the baby? I asked softly. He didn't answer. For a moment I was scared. Hector was strong, and probably bigger than me, and younger too, but I was a police officer.

Now I'm going to tie your paws and your snout and take you to the police station, I said. I think he smiled, but I'm not sure. You're more scared than I am, he said, and I'm pretty scared. I don't think so, I replied, you're not scared—you're sick, you're a disgusting predatory bastard. Hector laughed. *You're* scared, though, aren't you, he said, much more than your aunt Josephine was. You've heard of Josephine? I asked. I've heard of her, he said. Who hasn't? My aunt wasn't scared, I said, she might have been a poor crazy dreamer, but she wasn't scared.

You're wrong there; she was scared to death, he said, glancing sideways distractedly, as if we were surrounded by ghostly presences and he was discreetly seeking their approval. The members of her audience were scared to death as well, although they didn't know it. But she didn't die once and for all: she died every day at the center of fear, and in fear she came back to life. Words, I spat. Now lie face down while I tie your snout, I said, taking out the cord I had brought for that purpose. Hector snorted.

You've got no idea, he said. Do you think the crimes will stop if you arrest me? Do you think your bosses will give me a fair trial? They'll probably tear me to pieces in secret and dump my remains where predators will take them. You're a damn predator, I said. I'm a free rat, he replied impudently. I'm at home in fear and I know perfectly well where our people are headed. His words were so presumptuous I chose not to dignify them with an answer. Instead I said, You're young. Maybe there's a way to cure you. We don't kill our own kind. And who's going to cure you, Pepe? he asked. And your bosses? Where are the doctors to cure them? Lie face down, I said. Hector stared at me; I dropped the cord. Our bodies locked in a fight to the death.

After ten eternal-seeming minutes, he lay beside me, lifeless, his neck crushed by a bite. As for me, my back was covered with wounds, my snout was torn open, and I couldn't see anything out of my left eye. I took his body back to the station. The few rats I encountered no doubt supposed that Hector had been the victim of a predator. I left his body in the morgue and went to find the coroner. It's all solved now, were the first words I could articulate. Then I slumped to the ground and waited. The coroner examined my wounds and sewed up my snout and my eyelid. As he was attending to me, he asked how it had happened. I found the killer, I said. I stopped him; we fought. The coroner said he had to call the commissioner. He clicked his tongue and a thin, sleepy-looking adolescent emerged from the darkness. I assumed he was a medical student. The coroner told him to go to the commissioner's place and tell him that the coroner and Pepe the Cop were waiting for him at the station. The adolescent nodded and disappeared. Then the coroner and I went to the morgue.

Hector's body was lying there and his coat was beginning to lose its gloss. It was just another body now, one among many. While the coroner was examining it, I took a nap in a corner. I was woken by the commissioner's voice and a couple of shoves. Get up, Pepe, said the coroner. I followed them. The commissioner and the coroner scurried down tunnels that were unfamiliar to me. I followed them, half asleep, watching their tails, with an intense burning pain in my back. Soon we came to an empty burrow. There, on a kind of throne, or maybe it was a cradle, I saw a seething shadow. The commissioner and the coroner told me to go forward.

Tell me the story, said a voice that was many voices, emerging from the darkness. At first I was terrified and shrank away, but then I realized that it was a very old queen rat—several rats, that is, whose tails had become knotted in early childhood, which rendered them unfit for work, but endowed them, instead, with the requisite wisdom to advise our people in critical situations. So I told the story from beginning to end, and tried to make my words dispassionate and objective, as if I were writing a report. When I finished, the voice that was many voices emerging from the darkness asked me if I was the nephew of Josephine the Singer. That's correct, I said. We were born when Josephine was still alive, said the queen rat, shifting herselves laboriously. I could just make out a huge dark ball dotted with little eyes dimmed by age. The queen rat, I conjectured, was fat, and a build-up of filth had immobilized her hind paws. An anomaly, she said. It took me a while to realize that she was referring to Hector. A poison that shall not spell the end of life for us, she said: a kind of lunatic, an individualist. There's something I don't understand, I said. The commissioner touched me on the shoulder with his paw, as if to stop me from speaking, but the queen rat asked me to explain what it was that I didn't understand. Why did he let the baby die of hunger, instead of ripping his throat open, as he did with the other victims? For a few seconds all I could hear from the seething shadow was a sound of sighing.

Maybe, she said after a while, he wanted to witness the

process of death from beginning to end, without intervening or intervening as little as possible. And, after another interminable silence, she added: We must remember that he was insane, that we are in the realm of the monstrous—rats do not kill rats.

I hung my head and stayed there, I don't know for how long. I might even have fallen asleep. Suddenly I felt the commissioner's paw on my shoulder again, and heard his voice ordering me to follow him. We went back the way we had come, in silence. Just as I had feared, Hector's body had disappeared from the morgue. I asked where it was. In the belly of some predator, I hope, said the commissioner. Then I was told what I had already guessed. It was strictly forbidden to talk about Hector with anyone. The case was closed, and the best thing for me to do was to forget about him and get on with my life and my work.

I didn't feel like sleeping at the station that night, so I found myself a place in a burrow full of tough, grimy rats, and when I woke up I was alone. That night I dreamed that an unknown virus had infected our people. Rats are capable of killing rats. The sentence echoed in my cranial cavity until I woke. I knew that nothing would ever be the same again. I knew it was only a question of time. Our capacity to adapt to the environment, our hardworking nature, our long collective march toward a happiness that, deep down, we knew to be illusory, but which had served as a pretext, a setting, a backdrop for our daily acts of heroism, all these were condemned to disappear, which meant that we, as a people, were condemned to disappear as well.

I went back to my daily rounds; there was nothing else I

could do. A police officer was killed and torn to pieces by a predator; there were several fatalities as a result of more poisoning from the outside; a number of tunnels were flooded. One night, however, I yielded to the fever that was consuming my body and returned to the dead sewers.

I'm not sure whether that sewer was one of those in which I'd found a victim, or even if I'd been there before. All dead sewers are the same, in the end. I spent a long time in there, hiding, waiting. Nothing. Only distant noises, splashes: I couldn't say what caused them. When I returned to the station, with red eyes from my long vigil, I found some rats who swore they'd seen a pair of weasels in the tunnels nearby. There was a new police officer with them. He looked at me, waiting for some kind of sign. The weasels had cornered three rats and several young in the end of a tunnel. If we wait for backup it'll be too late, said the new officer.

Too late for what? I asked, yawning. For the young and their guardians, he replied. It's already too late, I thought, for everything. I also thought: When did it become too late? Was it in the time of my aunt Josephine? Or a hundred years before that? Or a thousand, three thousand years before? Weren't we damned right from the origin of our species? The officer was watching me, waiting for a cue. He was young and he couldn't have been on the job for more than a week. Some of the rats around us were whispering, others were pressing their ears to the walls of the tunnel; most of them, it was all they could do to stop themselves from shaking and running away. What do you suggest? I asked. We do it by the book, replied the officer, we go into the tunnel and rescue the young.

Have you ever taken on a weasel? Are you ready to be

torn apart by a weasel? I asked. I know how to fight, Pepe, he replied. There was nothing much left to say, so I got up and told him to stay behind me. The tunnel was black and stank of weasel, but I know how to move in the dark. Two rats came forward as volunteers and followed us.

ÁLVARO ROUSSELOT'S JOURNEY

for Carmen Pérez de Vega

Although it may not warrant an eminent place in the annals of literary mystery, the curious case of Álvaro Rousselot is worthy of attention, for a few minutes at least.

Keen readers of mid-twentieth-century Argentine literature, who do exist, albeit not in great numbers, will no doubt remember that Rousselot was a skilled narrator and an abundant inventor of original plots, a sound stylist in literary Spanish, but not averse to the use of Buenos Aires slang or *lunfardo*, when the story required it (as was often the case), though never in a mannered way, at least not for those of us who count ourselves among his faithful readers.

The action of that sinister and eminently sardonic character Time has, however, prompted a reconsideration of Rousselot's apparent simplicity. Perhaps he was complicated. By which I mean *much* more complicated than we had imagined. But there is an alternative explanation: perhaps he was simply another victim of chance.

Such cases are not unusual among lovers of literature. In fact, they are not unusual among lovers of anything. In the end we all fall victim to the object of our adoration, perhaps because passion runs its course more swiftly than other human emotions, perhaps as a result of excessive familiarity with the object of desire.

In any case, Rousselot loved literature as much as any Argentine writer of his generation, or of the preceding and following generations, which is to say that his love was somewhat disillusioned. What I mean is that he was not especially different from the others, his peers—he knew the same torments and moments of joy—yet nothing even remotely similar happened to any of them.

At this point it could be objected, quite reasonably, that the others were destined for hells or singularities of their own. Angela Caputo, for example, killed herself in an unimaginable manner: no one who had read her poems, with their ambivalently childish atmosphere, could have predicted such an atrocious death, stage-managed down to the finest detail to maximize the terrifying effect. Or Sánchez Brady, whose texts were hermetic and whose life was cut short by the military regime in the seventies, when he had passed the age of fifty and lost interest in literature and the world in general.

Paradoxical deaths and destinies, yet they do not eclipse the case of Rousselot, the enigma that imperceptibly enveloped his life, the sense that his work, his writing, stood near or on the edge or the brink of something he knew almost nothing about.

His story can be recounted simply, perhaps because, in the final analysis, it is a simple story. In 1950, at the age of thirty, Rousselot published his first book, a novel about daily life in a remote Patagonian penitentiary, under the rather laconic title *Solitude*. Not surprisingly, the book relates numerous confessions about past lives and fleeting moments of happiness; it also relates numerous acts of violence. Halfway through, it becomes apparent that most of the characters are dead. With only thirty pages left to go, it is suddenly obvious that they are *all* dead, except for one, but the identity of that single living character is never revealed. The book was not much of a success in Buenos Aires, selling less than a thousand copies, but, thanks to some friends, Rousselot had the pleasure of seeing a well-respected publisher bring out a French edition in 1954. *Solitude* became *Nights on the Pampas* in the land of Victor Hugo, where it made little impact, except on two critics, one of whom reviewed it warmly, while the other was perhaps excessively enthusiastic; then it vanished into the limbo of remote shelves and overloaded tables in secondhand bookstores.

At the end of 1957, however, a film entitled *Lost Voices* was released; it was directed by a Frenchman named Guy Morini, and for anyone who had read *Solitude*, it was clearly a clever adaptation of Rousselot's book. Morini's film began and ended altogether differently, but its stem or middle section corresponded exactly to the novel. It would, I think, be impossible to recapture Rousselot's feeling of stunned amazement in the dark, half-empty Buenos Aires cinema where he first saw the Frenchman's film. Naturally, he considered himself a victim of plagiarism. As the days went by, other explanations occurred to him, but he kept coming back to the idea that his work had been plagiarized. Of the friends who were informed and went to see the film, half were in favor of suing the production company, while the others were inclined to think, more or less resignedly, that these things happen—think of Brahms. By that time, Rousselot had already published a second novel, *The Archives of the Calle Peru*, a detective story, with a plot that revolved around the appearance of three bodies in three different places in Buenos Aires: the first two victims had been killed by the third, the victim in turn of an unknown assailant.

This second novel was not what one might have expected from the author of *Solitude*, but the critics received it well, although it is perhaps the least successful of Rousselot's works. When Morini's film came out in Buenos Aires, *The Archives of the Calle Peru* had already been kicking around the city's bookshops for almost a year, and Rousselot had married María Eugenia Carrasco, a young woman who moved in the capital's literary circles, and he had recently taken a job with the law firm Zimmerman & Gurruchaga.

Rousselot's life was orderly: he got up at six in the morning and wrote or tried to write until eight, at which time he interrupted his commerce with the muses, took a shower, and rushed off to the office, where he arrived at around ten to nine. He spent most mornings in court or going through files. At two in the afternoon, he returned home, had lunch with his wife, and then went back to the office for the afternoon. At seven, he would have a drink with some of his legal colleagues, and by eight, at the latest, he was back home, where Mrs. Rousselot, as she now was, had his dinner ready, after which Rousselot would read, while María Eugenia listened to the radio. On Saturdays and Sundays he wrote for a little longer, and went out at night, unaccompanied by his wife, to see his literary friends.

The release of *Lost Voices* brought him a degree of notoriety beyond his circle of associates. His best friend at the law firm, who was not particularly interested in literature, advised him to sue Morini for breach of copyright. Having thought it over carefully, Rousselot decided not to do anything. After *The Archives of the Calle Peru*, he published a slim volume of stories, and then, almost immediately, his third novel, *Life of a Newlywed*, in which, as the title suggests, he recounted a man's first months of married life, and how, as the days go by, the man comes to realize that he has made a terrible mistake: not only is the woman he thought he knew a stranger, she is also a kind of monster who threatens his mental balance and even his physical safety. And yet the guy loves her (or rather discovers that he is physically attracted to her in a way that he hadn't been before), so he holds on for as long as he can before fleeing.

The book was, obviously, meant to be humorous, and was taken as such by the reading public, to the surprise of Rousselot and his publisher. It had to be reprinted after three months, and within a year more than fifteen thousand copies had been sold. From one day to the next, Rousselot's name soared from comfortable semi-obscurity to provisional stardom. He took it in stride. With the windfall earnings, he treated himself, his wife, and his sister-in-law to a vacation in Punta del Este, which he spent surreptitiously reading *In Search of Lost Time*, a book he had always pretended to have read. While Maria Eugenia and her sister lolled about on the seashore, he strove to redeem that lie, but above all to fill the gap left by his ignorance of France's most celebrated novelist.

He would have been better off reading the Kabbalists. Seven months after his vacation in Punta del Este, before

Life of a Newlywed had come out in French, Morini's new film, *The Shape of the Day*, opened in Buenos Aires. It was exactly like *Life of a Newlywed* but better, that is, revised and considerably extended, much as Morini had done with *Lost Voices*, compressing the novel's plot into the central part of the film, while the beginning and the end served as commentaries on the main story (or ways into and out of it, or digressions leading nowhere, or simply—and here lay the charm of the procedure—delicately filmed scenes from the lives of the minor characters).

This time, Rousselot was extremely aggrieved. His case against Morini was the talk of the Argentinean literary world for a week or so. And yet, when everyone presumed that he would take swift legal action for breach of copyright, he decided, to the dismay of those who had expected him to adopt a stronger and more decisive stance, that he would do nothing. Few could really understand his reaction. He did not protest, or appeal to the honor and integrity of the artist. After his initial surprise and indignation, Rousselot simply opted not to act, at least not legally. He waited. Something inside him, which could perhaps, without too great a risk of error, be called the writer's spirit, trapped him in a limbo of apparent passivity, and began to harden or change him, or prepare him for future surprises.

In other respects his life as a writer and as a man had already changed as much as he could reasonably have hoped, or more: his books were well reviewed and widely read, they even supplemented his income, and his family life was suddenly enriched by the news that María Eugenia was going to be a mother. When Morini's third film came to Buenos Aires,

Rousselot stayed home for a week, resisting the temptation to rush to the cinema like a man possessed. He also instructed his friends not to tell him the plot. At first he thought he would not go to see the film. But after a week it was too much for him, and one night, having kissed his baby son and entrusted him to the nanny's care as if he were leaving for a war and would never return, he stepped out, resignedly, arm in arm with his wife, and went to the cinema.

Morini's film was called *The Vanished Woman*, and had nothing in common with any of Rousselot's works, or with either of Morini's previous films. As they left the cinema, María Eugenia said she thought it was bad and boring. Álvaro Rousselot kept his opinion to himself, but he agreed. A few months later, he published his next novel, the longest yet (206 pages), entitled *The Juggler's Family*, in which he departed from the style that had characterized his work up till then, with its elements of fantasy and crime fiction, and experimented with what, at a stretch, could be called the choral or polyphonic novel. It wasn't a form that came naturally to him, and seemed rather forced, but the book was redeemed by other features: the decency and simplicity of the characters, a naturalism that elegantly avoided the clichés of the naturalist novel, and the stories themselves, which were slight and resolute, joyful and pointless, and captured the indomitable Argentine spirit.

The Juggler's Family was, without doubt, Rousselot's greatest success, the book that brought all the others back into print, and his triumph was consummated by the Municipal Literary Award, presented at a ceremony in the course of which he was described as one of the five rising stars among the nation's younger writers. But that is another story. It is common knowledge that the rising stars of any literary world are like flowers that bloom and fade in a day; and whether the day is literal and brief or stretches out over ten or twenty years, it must eventually come to an end.

The French, who distrust our municipal literary awards on principle, were slow to translate and publish *The Juggler's Family*. By then, fashions in Latin American fiction had shifted north to more tropical climes. When the novel came out in Paris, Morini had already made his fourth and fifth films, a conventional but engaging French detective story and a turkey about a supposedly amusing family vacation in Saint-Tropez.

Both films were released in Argentina, and Rousselot was relieved to discover that neither bore the slightest resemblance to anything he had written. It was as if Morini had distanced himself from Rousselot, or, under pressure from creditors and swept up in the whirlwind of the movie business, had neglected the relationship. After relief came sadness. For a few days Rousselot was even preoccupied by the thought that he had lost his best reader, the reader for whom he had really been writing, the only one who was capable of fully responding to his work. He tried to get in touch with his translators, but they were busy with other books and other authors, and replied to his letters with polite and evasive phrases. One of them had never seen any of Morini's films. The other had seen one of the films in question but hadn't translated the corresponding book (or even read it, to judge from his letter).

When Rousselot asked his publishers in Paris if Morini might have had access to the manuscript of *Life of a Newlywed* before its publication, they weren't even surprised. They replied indifferently that many people had access to a manuscript at various stages prior to printing. Feeling embarrassed, Rousselot decided to stop annoying people with his letters and suspend his investigations until such time as he could finally go to Paris himself. A year later he was invited to a literary festival in Frankfurt.

The Argentine delegation was sizable and the journey was pleasant. Rousselot got to know two old Buenos Aires writers whom he considered his masters. He tried to help them in any way he could, offering to render the sort of little services one might expect from a secretary or a valet rather than a colleague. This behavior was condemned by a writer of his own generation, who called him obsequious and servile, but Rousselot was happy and paid no attention. The stay in Frankfurt was enjoyable, in spite of the weather, and Rousselot spent all his time with the pair of old writers.

The atmosphere of slightly artificial happiness was, in fact, largely Rousselot's own creation. He knew that when the festival was over, he would go on to Paris, while the others would return to Buenos Aires or take a short vacation somewhere in Europe. When the day of departure came and he went to the airport to see off the members of the delegation who were returning to Argentina, his eyes filled with tears. One of the old writers noticed and told him not to worry, they would see each other again soon, and the door of his house in Buenos Aires would always be open. But Rousselot couldn't understand what anyone was saying to him. He was on the brink of tears because he was afraid of being left on his own, and, above all, afraid of going to Paris and confronting the mystery awaiting him there.

The first thing he did, as soon as he had settled into a little hotel in Saint-Germain-des-Prés, was to call the translator of *Solitude* (*Nights on the Pampas*), unsuccessfully. The phone rang, but no one picked up, and when Rousselot went to the publisher's offices, they had no idea where the translator might be. To tell the truth, they had no idea who Rousselot was either, although he pointed out that they had published two of his books, *Nights on the Pampas* and *Life of a Newlywed.* Finally, a guy who must have been about fifty, and whose role in the company Rousselot never managed to ascertain, identified the visitor and, abruptly changing the topic, proceeded to inform him, in an absurdly serious tone, that the sales of his books had been very poor.

Rousselot then visited the publishers of *The Juggler's Family* (which Morini, it seemed, had never read) and made a half-hearted attempt to obtain the address of the translator they had employed, hoping that he would be able to put him in touch with the translators of *Nights on the Pampas* and *Life of a Newlywed.* This second publishing house was significantly smaller and seemed to be run by just two people: the woman who received Rousselot, whom he guessed was a secretary, and the publisher, a young guy, who greeted him with a smile and a hug, and insisted on speaking Spanish, although it was soon clear that his grasp of the language was tenuous. When asked why he wanted to speak with the translator of *The Juggler's Family*, Rousselot was at a loss for words, because he had just realized how absurd it was to think that any of his translators would be able to lead him to Morini. Nevertheless, encouraged by the publisher's warm welcome (and his readiness to listen, since he didn't seem to have anything better to do that morning), Rousselot decided to tell him the whole Morini story, from A to Z.

When he had finished, the publisher lit a cigarette, and paced up and down the office for a long time in silence, from one wall to the other and back, a distance of barely three yards. Rousselot waited, becoming increasingly nervous. Finally the publisher stopped in front of a glass-fronted bookcase full of manuscripts and asked Rousselot if it was his first time in Paris. Rather taken aback, Rousselot admitted that it was. Parisians are cannibals, said the publisher. Rousselot hastened to point out that he was not intending to take any kind of legal action against Morini; he only wanted to meet him and perhaps ask him how he'd come up with the plots of the two films in which he, Rousselot, had, so to speak, a particular interest. The publisher burst into uproarious laughter. It's all about money here, he said, ever since Camus. Rousselot looked at him, bewildered. He didn't know whether the publisher meant that idealism had died with Camus, and money was now the prime concern, or that Camus had established the law of supply and demand among artists and intellectuals.

I'm not interested in money, said Rousselot quietly. Nor am I, my poor friend, said the publisher, and look where it's got me.

They parted with the understanding that Rousselot would call the publisher and arrange to have dinner one night. He spent the rest of the day sightseeing. He went to the Louvre and the Eiffel Tower; he ate in a restaurant in the Latin Quarter, and visited a couple of secondhand bookshops. That night, from his hotel, he called an Argentine writer he had known back in Buenos Aires and who now lived in Paris.

They weren't exactly friends, but Rousselot admired his work and had been instrumental in getting a number of his pieces published in a Buenos Aires magazine.

The Argentine writer was called Riquelme and he was happy to hear from Rousselot. Rousselot wanted to arrange to meet up some time during the week, perhaps for lunch or dinner, but Riquelme wouldn't hear of it and asked him where he was calling from. Rousselot told him the name of his hotel and mentioned that he was thinking of going to bed. Riquelme said, Don't even think of getting into your pajamas, I'll be right there; it's my treat tonight. Rousselot was overwhelmed, powerless to resist. He hadn't seen Riquelme for years and, waiting in the hotel lobby, tried to remember what he looked like. He had blond hair and a round, broad face with a ruddy complexion; he was short. It had been a while since Rousselot had read any of his work.

When Riquelme finally appeared, Rousselot hardly recognized him: he seemed taller, not so blond, and he was wearing glasses. The night was rich in confessions and revelations. Rousselot told his friend what he had told his French publisher that morning, and Riquelme told Rousselot that he was writing the great Argentine novel of the twentieth century. He had passed the eight-hundred-page mark, and hoped to finish it in less than three years. Although Rousselot prudently refrained from asking about the plot, Riquelme explained several sections of his book in detail. They visited various bars and clubs. At some point during the night, Rousselot realized that both he and Riquelme were behaving like adolescents. At first this embarrassed him, but then he surrendered to the situation, happy to know that his hotel was there at the end of the night, his hotel room and the word *hotel*, which in that instant seemed a miraculous (that is to say instantaneous) incarnation of risk and freedom.

He drank a lot. On waking, he discovered a woman beside him. The woman's name was Simone and she was a prostitute. They had breakfast together in a café near the hotel. Simone liked to talk, so Rousselot discovered that she didn't have a pimp, because a pimp will always rip you off, that she had just turned twenty-eight, and that she liked watching movies. Since he wasn't interested in the world of Parisian pimps and Simone's age didn't seem a fruitful topic of conversation, they started talking about movies. She liked French cinema, and before long they got onto Morini. His first films were very good, in Simone's opinion. Rousselot could have kissed her when she said that.

At two in the afternoon they returned to the hotel and didn't reemerge until dinnertime. It would probably be true to say that Rousselot had never felt so good in his life. He wanted to write, and eat, and go out dancing with Simone, and wander aimlessly through the streets of the Left Bank. In fact, he felt so good that during the meal, shortly before they ordered dessert, he explained the reason for his trip to Paris. To Rousselot's surprise, Simone was not at all surprised by the revelation that he was a writer or that Morini had plagiarized or copied his work, or freely adapted two of his novels to make his two best films.

Things like that do happen, was her laconic response, and even stranger things. Then, point-blank, she asked him if he was married. The answer was implicit in the question, and with a resigned gesture Rousselot showed her the gold ring constricting his finger in that moment as it never had before. And do you have children? asked Simone. A little boy, said Rousselot with a tenderness engendered by the mental image of his offspring. And he added, He looks just like me. Then Simone asked him to keep her company on the way home. In the taxi, neither of them said a word; both looked out of their windows at the unpredictable spills of bright and dark, which made the City of Light seem like a medieval Russian city, or at least like the images of such cities that Soviet directors used to offer for public consumption every now and then in their films. Finally the taxi pulled up in front of a four-story building and Simone invited him to come in. Rousselot wondered whether he should, and then he remembered that he hadn't paid her. Shamefaced, he got out of the taxi without worrying about how he would get back to his hotel (there didn't seem to be many taxis in that neighborhood). Before going into the building, he held out a bunch of uncounted bills, which Simone put into her handbag, without counting them either.

The building didn't have an elevator. By the time they reached the fourth floor, Rousselot was out of breath. In the dimly lit living room an old woman was drinking a whitish-colored liqueur. In response to a sign from Simone, Rousselot sat down next to the old woman, who produced a glass and filled it with that appalling liquid, while Simone vanished through one of the doors, then reappeared after a while and summoned him with a gesture. What now? thought Rousselot.

The room was small; it contained a bed in which a child was sleeping. My son, said Simone. He's lovely, said Rousselot. And he was a pretty child, but perhaps that was only because he was sleeping. He had blond hair, which was rather too long, and resembled his mother, although Rousselot noted that there was already something thoroughly manly about his childish features. When he went back to the living room, Simone was paying the old woman, who then took her leave of madame, and even wished her visitor an effusive good night, calling him *sir*. Rousselot was thinking that the day had been eventful enough and that it was time to leave when Simone said he could spend the night with her, if he liked. But you can't sleep in my bed, she said; she didn't want her son to see her in bed with a stranger. So they made love in Simone's room, and then Rousselot went out into the living room, lay down on the couch, and fell asleep.

He spent the next day en famille, so to speak. The little boy's name was Marc; Rousselot found him to be very bright (as well as speaking better French than he did). The novelist spared no expense: they had breakfast in the center of Paris, went to a park, had lunch in a restaurant on the Rue de Verneuil, which he had been told about in Buenos Aires, then they went rowing on a lake, and finally they visited a supermarket where Simone bought all the ingredients for a proper French meal. They took taxis everywhere. As they waited for ice creams on a café terrace on the Boulevard Saint-Germain, Rousselot recognized a pair of famous writers. He admired them from a distance. Simone asked him if he knew them. He said no, but he was a passionate reader of their books. Then go and ask them for an autograph, she said.

At first it seemed a perfectly reasonable idea, the natural thing to do, but at the last moment Rousselot decided that he didn't have the right to annoy anyone, least of all people he'd always admired. That night he slept in Simone's bed; they covered each other's mouths to stop their moans waking the child, and made love for hours, violently at times, as if loving each other were the only thing they knew how to do. The next day he returned to his hotel before the child woke up.

His suitcase had not been put out in the street as he had feared, and no one was surprised to see him appear out of nowhere, like a ghost. At reception there were two messages from Riquelme. The first was to say he had found out how to locate Morini. The second was to ask if Rousselot was still interested in meeting him.

He showered, shaved, brushed his teeth (a horrifying experience), put on clean clothes, and called Riquelme. They talked for a long time. Riquelme told him that a friend of his, a Spanish journalist, knew another journalist, a Frenchman, who was a freelance movie, theater, and music critic. The French journalist had been a friend of Morini's and still had his telephone number. When the Spaniard had asked for the number, the Frenchman had given it to him without a second thought. Then Riquelme and the Spanish journalist had called Morini's number without getting their hopes up, and were amazed when the woman who answered told them that they had indeed reached the director's residence.

Now all they had to do was set up a meeting (at which Riquelme and the Spanish journalist wanted to be present) on some pretext—anything, for example an interview for an Argentinean newspaper . . . with a surprise ending. What do you mean a surprise ending? shouted Rousselot. That's when the bogus journalist reveals his true identity and confronts the plagiarist, Riquelme replied.

That night, as Rousselot was taking photographs more or

less at random on the banks of the Seine, a bum came up and asked him for some change. Rousselot offered him a bill if he would consent to be photographed. The bum agreed, and for a while they walked along together in silence, stopping every now and then to allow the Argentine writer to move off to an appropriate distance and take a photo. On the third occasion the bum suggested a pose, which Rousselot accepted without demur. The writer took eight photos in all: the bum on his knees with his arms stretched out to the sides, and in other poses, such as pretending to sleep on a bench, thoughtfully watching the river flow by, or smiling and waving his hand. When the photo session was over, Rousselot gave him two bills and all the coins in his pocket, and then the pair of them stood there together, as if there were something more to be said but neither of them dared say it. Where are you from? the bum asked. Buenos Aires, Argentina, replied Rousselot. What a coincidence, said the bum in Spanish, I'm Argentine too. Rousselot was not at all surprised by this revelation. The bum began to hum a tango, then told him that in Europe, where he'd been living for more than fifteen years, he had found happiness and even some wisdom now and then. Rousselot realized that the bum had started using the familiar form of address, which he hadn't done when they were speaking in French. Even his voice, the tone of his voice, seemed to have changed. Rousselot felt a deep sadness overwhelming him, as if he knew that, come the end of the day, he would have to look into an abyss. The bum noticed and asked him what he was worried about.

Nothing, a girl, said Rousselot, trying to adopt the same tone as his compatriot. Then he said a rather hurried goodbye and, as he was climbing the stairs, he heard the bum's voice telling him that death was the only sure thing. My name is Enzo Cherubini and I'm telling you, death is the only sure thing there is. When Rousselot turned around, the bum was walking off in the opposite direction.

That night he called Simone but she wasn't home. He talked for a while with the old woman who looked after the child, then hung up. At ten, Riquelme came visiting. Reluctant to go out, Rousselot said he felt feverish and nauseous, but his excuses were futile. Sadly, he came to the realization that Paris had transformed his colleague into a force of nature it was futile to resist. That night they dined in a little restaurant with a charcoal grill in the Rue Racine, where they were joined by the Spanish journalist, named Paco Morral, who liked to imitate the Buenos Aires accent, very badly, and believed that Spanish cinema was far better than French cinema, much denser, an opinion shared by Riquelme.

The meal went on and on, and Rousselot began to feel ill. When he returned to his hotel at four in the morning, he was running a fever and began to vomit. He woke shortly before midday with the feeling that he had lived in Paris for many years. He went through the pockets of his jacket looking for the cell phone that he had managed to extract from Riquelme, and called Morini. A woman, the one who had previously spoken to Riquelme, he supposed, picked up the receiver and told him that Monsieur Morini had left that morning to spend a few days with his parents. Rousselot's first thought was that she was lying, or that before his hurried departure, the director had lied to her. He said he was an Argentine journalist who wanted to interview Morini for a well-known magazine with a big circulation, widely read all over Latin America, from Argentina to Mexico. The only problem, he alleged, was that he had limited time, since he had to fly home in a couple of days. Humbly he asked for the address of Morini's parents. He didn't have to insist. The woman listened politely, then gave him the name of a village in Normandy, followed by a street and a number.

Rousselot thanked her, then called Simone. No one was home. Suddenly he realized that he didn't even know what day it was. He thought of asking one of the hotel staff but felt embarrassed. He called Riquelme. A hoarse voice answered on the other end of the line. Rousselot asked him about the village where Morini's parents lived: Did he know where it was? Who's Morini? asked Riquelme. Rousselot had to remind him and explain part of the story again. No idea, said Riquelme, and hung up. After feeling annoyed for a while, Rousselot told himself it was better that way, if Riquelme lost interest in the whole business. Then he packed his suitcase and went to the train station.

The trip to Normandy gave him time to go back over what he had done since arriving in Paris. An absolute zero lit up in his mind, then delicately disappeared forever. The train stopped in Rouen. Other Argentines, and Rousselot himself in other circumstances, would have set off at once to explore the town, like bloodhounds following the scent of Flaubert. But he didn't even leave the station; he waited twenty minutes for the train to Caen, thinking of Simone, who personified the grace of French women, and of Riquelme and his odd journalist friend: in the end, both of them were more interested in rummaging through their own failures than in discovering someone else's story, however singular it might be, and perhaps that wasn't so unusual. People are only interested in themselves, he concluded gravely.

From Caen, he took a taxi to Le Hamel. He was surprised to find that the address he had been given in Paris corresponded to a hotel. The hotel had four stories and was not without a certain charm, but it was shut until the beginning of the season. For half an hour Rousselot walked around in the vicinity, wondering if the woman who lived with Morini had sent him on a wild goose chase, until eventually he began to feel tired and headed for the port. In a bar he was told that he'd be very lucky to find a hotel open in Le Hamel. The patron, a cadaverously pale guy with red hair, suggested he go to Arromanches, unless he wanted to sleep in one of the auberges that stayed open all year round. Rousselot thanked him and went looking for a taxi.

He booked into the best hotel he could find in Arromanches, a pile made of brick, stone, and wood, which creaked in the gusting wind. Tonight I will dream of Proust, he thought. Then he called Simone's place and talked to the old lady who looked after her child. Madame won't be home until after four; she has an orgy tonight, said the woman. A what? asked Rousselot. The woman repeated the sentence. My God, thought Rousselot, and hung up without saying goodbye. To make things worse, that night he didn't dream of Proust but of Buenos Aires, where thousands of Riquelmes had taken up residence in the Argentine PEN Club, all armed with tickets to Paris, all shouting, all cursing a name, the name of someone or something, but Rousselot couldn't hear it properly; it was like a tongue twister or a password they were trying to keep secret although it was gnawing their insides away.

The next morning, at breakfast, he was stunned to discover that he had no money left. Le Hamel was three or four kilometers from Arromanches; he decided to walk. To lift his spirits, he told himself that on D-Day the English soldiers had landed on those beaches. But his spirits remained as low as could be, and although he had thought it might take half an hour, in the end it took him more than twice that time to reach Le Hamel. On the way he started doing sums, remembering how much money he had brought with him to Europe, how much he'd had left when he arrived in Paris, how much he had spent on meals, on Simone (quite a lot, he thought, melancholically), on Riquelme, on taxis (they've been ripping me off the whole time!), and wondering whether he could have been robbed at some point without realizing. The only people who could have done that, he concluded gallantly, were the Spanish journalist and Riquelme. And the idea didn't seem preposterous in those surroundings where so many lives had been lost.

He observed Morini's hotel from the beach. By that stage, anyone else would have given up. For anyone else, circling around that hotel would have been as good as admitting to idiocy, or to a sort of degradation that Rousselot thought of as Parisian, or cinematic, or even literary, although for him the word *literary* retained all its original luster, or some of it, at least. In his situation, anyone else would have been calling the Argentine embassy, inventing a credible lie, and borrowing some money to pay for the hotel. But, instead of gritting his teeth and making the phone calls, Rousselot rang the hotel's doorbell and was not surprised to hear the voice of an old woman who, leaning out of one of the windows on the second floor, asked him what he wanted and was not surprised by his reply: I need to see your son. Then the old woman disappeared, and Rousselot waited by the door for what seemed like an eternity.

He kept checking his pulse and touching his forehead to see if he had a fever. When the door finally opened, he saw a lean, rather swarthy face, with large bags under the eyes; it was, he judged, the face of a degenerate, and it was vaguely familiar. Morini invited him in. My parents, he said, have been working as caretakers of this hotel for more than thirty years. They sat down in the lobby, where the armchairs were protected from dust by enormous sheets embroidered with the hotel's monogram. On one wall Rousselot saw an oil painting of the beaches of Le Hamel, with bathers in belle époque costumes, while opposite, a collection of portraits of famous guests (or so he supposed) observed them from a zone infiltrated by mist. He shivered. I am Álvaro Rousselot, he said, the author of *Solitude*—I mean, the author of *Nights on the Pampas*.

It took a few seconds for Morini to react, but then he leaped to his feet, let out a cry of terror, and disappeared down a corridor. Such a spectacular response was the last thing Rousselot had been expecting. He remained seated, lit a cigarette (the ash dropped progressively onto the carpet), and thought sadly of Simone and her son, and a café in Paris that served the best croissants he had ever tasted in his life.

Then he stood up and started calling Morini. Guy, he called, rather hesitantly, Guy, Guy, Guy.

Rousselot found him in an attic where the hotel's cleaning equipment was piled. Morini had opened the window and seemed to be hypnotized by the garden that surrounded the building, and by the neighboring garden, which belonged to a private residence, and was visible, in part, through dark latticework. Rousselot walked over and patted him on the back. Morini seemed smaller and more fragile than before. For a while they both stood there looking at one garden, then the other. Then Rousselot wrote the address of his hotel in Paris and the address of the hotel where he was currently staying on a piece of paper and slipped it into the director's trouser pocket. He felt he had committed a reprehensible act, executed a reprehensible gesture, but then, as he was walking back to Arromanches, everything he had done in Paris, every gesture and action, seemed reprehensible, futile, senseless, and even ridiculous. I should kill myself, he thought as he walked along the seashore.

Back in Arromanches, he did what any sensible man would have done as soon as he realized that his money had run out. He rang Simone, explained the situation, and asked her for a loan. The first thing Simone said was that she didn't want a pimp, to which Rousselot replied that he was asking for a *loan*, and that he was planning to repay it with thirty-percent interest, but then they both started laughing and Simone told him not to do anything, just stay put in the hotel, and in a few hours, as soon as she could borrow a car from one of her friends, she'd come and get him. She also called him *chéri* a few times, to which he responded by using the word *chérie*, which had never seemed so tender. For the rest of the day Rousselot felt that he really was an Argentine writer, something he had begun to doubt over the previous days, or perhaps the previous years, partly because he was unsure of himself, but also because he was unsure about the possibility of an Argentine literature.

TWO CATHOLIC TALES

I. THE VOCATION

1. I was seventeen years old and my days, and I mean all of them, were a continual shuddering. I had no distractions; nothing could dissipate the anxiety that kept building up inside me. I was living like an interloping extra in scenes from the passion of St. Vincent. St. Vincent—deacon to Bishop Valero, tortured by the governor Dacian in the year 304—have pity on me! **2.** Sometimes I talked with Juanito. Not just sometimes. Often. We sat in armchairs at his place and talked about movies. Juanito liked Gary Cooper. Elegance, temperance, integrity, courage, he used to say. Temperance? Courage? I knew what lay behind his certitudes, and would have liked to spit them back in his face, but instead I dug my fingernails into the armrests and bit my lip when he wasn't looking and even closed my eyes and pretended to be meditating on his words. But I wasn't meditating. Not at all: images of the martyrdom of St. Vincent were flashing in my mind like magic lantern slides. **3.** First he is tied to an X-shaped wooden cross and they tear at his flesh with hooks and dislocate his limbs. Then he is subjected to torture by fire, roasted on a grill over hot coals. And then he's a captive in a dungeon where the ground is covered with shards of glass and pottery. And then a crow keeps watch over the martyr's corpse, abandoned in a wasteland, and fends off a ravening wolf. And then the saint's body is cast into the sea from a boat, a millstone tied around his neck. And then the waves wash the body up on the coast, and there it is piously buried by a matron and other Christians. **4.** Sometimes I used to feel dizzy. Nauseous. Juanito would talk about the last film we had seen and I would nod and realize that I was drowning, as if the armchairs were at the bottom of a very deep lake. I could remember the movie theater, I could remember buying the tickets, but I simply couldn't remember the scenes that my friend (my one and only friend!) was talking about, as if the lake-floor darkness had infiltrated everything. If I open my mouth, water will come in. If I breathe, water will come in. If I stay alive, water will come in and flood my lungs forever and ever. **5.** Sometimes Juanito's mother would come into the room and ask me personal questions. How my studies were going, what book I was reading, if I'd been to the circus that had just set up on the outskirts of the city. Juanito's mother was always very elegantly dressed, and, like us, she was addicted to the movies. **6.** Once I dreamed of her, once I opened the door of her bedroom, and instead of seeing a bed, a dresser, and a closet, I saw an empty room with a red brick floor, and that was just the antechamber of a very, very long corridor, like the highway tunnel that goes through the mountains and then on toward France, except that in this case the tunnel wasn't on a mountain highway but in the bedroom of my best friend's mother. I have to keep reminding myself: Juanito's my best friend. And, as opposed to a normal tunnel, this one seemed to be suspended in a very fragile kind of silence, like the silence of the second half of January or the first half of February. **7.** Unspeakable acts, fateful nights. I recited the formula to Juanito. Unspeakable acts? Fateful nights? Is the act unspeakable because the night is fateful, or is the night fateful because the act is unspeakable? What sort of question is that? I asked, on the brink of tears. You're crazy. You don't understand anything, I said, looking out of the window. **8.** Juanito's father isn't tall but he cuts a dashing figure. He was in the army and during the war he was wounded a number of times. His medals are displayed on the wall of his study, in a glass-fronted case. He didn't know anyone when he first came to the city, Juanito says, and people were either afraid of him or jealous. After a few months here, he met my mother, Juanito says. They were engaged for five years. Then my father tied the knot. Sometimes my aunt talks about Juanito's father. According to her, he was a good, honest police chief. That's what people said, at least. If a maid was caught stealing from her employers, Juanito's father locked her up for three days without so much as a crust of bread. On the fourth day he would question her personally, and the maid would be quick to confess her sin, giving him the precise location of the jewels or the name of the laborer who had stolen them. Then the guards would arrest the man and lock him up, and Juanito's father would put the maid on a train and advise her not to come back. **9.** The whole village applauded this procedure, as if it were a sign of the police chief's intellectual distinction. **10.** When Juanito's father first arrived, the only people he knew socially were the regulars at the casino. Juanito's mother was seventeen years old and she was very blonde, to judge from a number of photos hanging unobtrusively around the house, much blonder than she is now, and she had been educated at the Heart of Mary, a school run by nuns in the northern part of the old fort. Juanito's father must have been about thirty. He still goes to the casino every afternoon, although he's retired now, and drinks a glass of cognac or coffee with a shot, and usually plays dice with the regulars. New regulars, not the regulars from the old days, but it's not so different, because of course they're all in awe of him. Juanito's older brother lives in Madrid, where he's a well-known lawyer. Juanito's sister is married and she lives in Madrid too. I'm the only one left in this damn house, Juanito says. And me! And me! **11.** Our city is shrinking every day. Sometimes I get the feeling that everyone is either leaving or shut up inside packing a suitcase. If I left, I wouldn't take a suitcase. Not even a few belongings wrapped up in a little bundle. Sometimes I put my head in my hands and listen to the rats running in the walls. St. Vincent, grant me strength. St. Vincent, grant me temperance. **12.** Do you want to be a saint? Juanito's mother asked me two years ago. Yes, ma'am. I think that's a very good idea, but you have to be very good. Are you? I try to be, ma'am. And a year ago, as I was walking along Avenida General Mola, Juanito's father said hello and then he stopped and asked if I was Encarnación's nephew. Yes, sir, I said. You're the one who wants to become a priest? I nodded and smiled. **13.** Why did I do that? What was that stupid, apologetic smile for? Why did I look away smiling like a moron? **14.** Humility. **15.** That's excellent, said Juanito's father. Fantastic. You have to study hard, don't you? I nodded and smiled. And cut down on the movies? Yes, sir, but I don't go to the movies much. **16.** I watched Juanito's father receding into the distance: old but still vigorous, he held himself straight and looked as if he were walking on tiptoes. I watched him go down the stairs that lead to the Calle de los Vidrieros; I watched him as he walked away without a moment's unsteadiness or hesitation, without looking into a single shop. Not like Juanito's mother, who was always looking in storefront windows, and sometimes she would go into the stores, and if you stayed outside, waiting for her, you could sometimes hear her laugh. If I open my mouth, water will come in. If I breathe, water will come in. If I stay alive, water will come in and flood my lungs forever and ever. **17.** And what are you going to be, dickhead? Juanito asked me. Be or do? I asked him back. Be, dickhead. Whatever God wants, I said. God puts us all in our rightful places, said my aunt. Our forefathers were good people. There were no soldiers in our family, but there were priests. Like who? I asked as I nodded off to sleep. My aunt grunted. I saw a square blanketed with snow, and I saw the farmers come with their produce, sweep the snow away, and wearily set up their market stalls. St. Vincent, for example, my aunt burst out. Deacon to the bishop of Zaragoza, who, in the year 304, anno Domini, though it might well have been 305, 306, 307, or 303, was arrested and taken to Valencia, where Dacian, the governor, submitted him to cruel tortures, as a result of which he died. **18.** Why do you think St. Vincent is dressed in red? I asked Juanito. No idea. Because all the Catholic martyrs wear a red garment, to identify them as martyrs. This boy's clever, said Father Zubieta. We were alone and Father Zubieta's study was bone-chillingly cold, and Father Zubieta or rather Father Zubieta's clothes smelled of a combination of dark tobacco and sour milk. If you decide to enter the seminary, the door is open. The vocation, the call, when it comes, can make you tremble, but let's not get carried away. Did I tremble? Did I feel the earth move? Did I experience the rapture of divine union? **19.** Let's not get carried away. Let's not get carried away. It's what the reds wear, said Juanito. The reds wear khaki, I said, green, with camouflage patterns. No, said Juanito, those red faggots wear red. Like whores. That piqued my curiosity. Like whores? Which whores, where? Well, here, for a start, said Juanito, and I guess in Madrid too. Here, in this city? Yes, said Juanito, and then he tried to change the subject. You mean there are whores even here, in this little city or town or godforsaken backwater? Well, yes, said Juanito. I thought your father had reformed them all. Reformed? Do you think my father's a priest or something? My father was a war hero and then a police commissioner. My father doesn't reform. He solves crimes. That's all. And where have you seen these whores? On Cerro del Moro, where they've always been, said Juanito. Good God. **20.** My aunt says that St. Vincent— Enough about your aunt and St. Vincent, your aunt is raving mad. How can you trace your family back to the year 300? Who's got a family that old? Not even the House of Alba. But after a while, he added: Your aunt's not a bad person; she's got a good heart, but her mind's not right. Shall we go to the movies this afternoon? They're showing a Clark Gable film. And Juanito's mother: Go on, go, I went two days ago and it's very entertaining. And Juanito: The thing is, he doesn't have any money. Juanito's mother: Well, you'll just have to lend him some. **21.** God have mercy on my soul. Sometimes I wish they'd all just die. My friend and his mother and his father and my aunt and all the neighbors and passersby and drivers who leave their cars parked by the river and even the poor innocent children who run around in the park beside the river. God have pity on my soul and make me better. Or unmake me. **22.** Anyway, if they all died, what would I do with so many bodies? How could I go on living in this city, or sub-city? Would I try to bury them all? Would I throw their bodies into the river? How much time would I have before their flesh began to rot and the stench became unbearable? Ah, snow. **23.** Snow covered the streets of our city. Before going into the cinema we bought roasted chestnuts and sugared almonds. We had our scarves up around our noses and Juanito was laughing and talking about adventures in the old Dutch East Indies. They didn't let anyone in with chestnuts—it was a question of basic hygiene—but they made an exception for Juanito. Gary Cooper would have been better in this role, said Juanito. Asia. The Chinese. Leper colonies. Mosquitoes. **24.** When we came out we went our separate ways in the Calle de los Cuchillos. I stood still in the falling snow and Juanito went running off home. Poor kid, I thought, but Juanito was only a year younger than me. When he disappeared from sight, I went up the Calle de los Toneleros to the Plaza del Sordo, and then I turned and followed the walls of the old fort, headed for Cerro del Moro. The snow reflected the light of the streetlamps, and, in a fleeting but also natural and even serene way, the old housefronts gathered the glamour of the past. I peered through a gap in the whitewash on a window and saw a tidy room, with the Sacred Heart of Jesus presiding on one of the walls. But I was blind and deaf and continued up the hill, on the dark side of the street so I wouldn't be recognized. When I reached the Plazuela del Cadalso, and only then, I realized that throughout the climb I hadn't come across a single person. In this weather, I thought, who would exchange the warmth of home for the freezing streets? It was already dark, and from the square you could see the lights of some of the neighborhoods and the bridges beyond the Plaza de Don Rodrigo and the river bending around and then continuing eastward. The stars were shining in the sky. I thought they looked like snowflakes. Suspended snowflakes, picked out by God to remain still in the firmament, but snowflakes all the same. **25.** I was starting to freeze. I decided to go back to my aunt's house and drink some hot chocolate or soup beside the heater. I felt weary and my head was spinning. I went back the way I'd come. Then I saw him. Just a shadow at first. **26.** But it wasn't a shadow, it was a monk. He could have been a Franciscan, judging from his habit. His thoughtful face was almost entirely obscured by a large hood. Why do I say thoughtful? Because he was looking at the ground. **27.** Where was he from? How'd he get there? I didn't know. Maybe he'd been administering the last rites to someone who was dying. Maybe he'd been visiting a sick child. Maybe he'd been supplying a destitute person with a frugal meal. In any case, he was walking without making the slightest sound. For a moment I thought it was an apparition. But soon I realized that the snow was muffling my own footfalls as well. **28.** He was barefoot. Noticing that was like being struck by lightning. We came down Cerro del Moro. When we passed the church of Santa Barbara, I saw him make the sign of the cross. His immaculate footprints shone in the snow like a message from God. I started crying. I would gladly have knelt down and kissed those crystalline prints—the answer for which I had waited so long—but I didn't, for fear he might disappear down some alley. We left the center. We crossed the Plaza Mayor, and then we crossed a bridge. The monk was walking at a steady pace, neither slowly nor quickly, as the Church herself should proceed. **29.** We followed the Avenida Sanjurjo, lined with plane trees, until we reached the train station. It was stifling inside. The monk went to the bathroom and then bought a ticket. When he came out of the bathroom, I noticed that he had put on a pair of shoes. His ankles were as slender as sticks. He went out onto the platform. I saw him sitting there, hanging his head, waiting and praying. I remained standing on the platform, shivering with cold, hidden by a pillar. When the train arrived, the monk jumped with surprising agility into one of the carriages. **30.** When I left, on my own, I looked for his prints in the snow, the footprints of his bare feet, but I could find no trace of them.

II. CHANCE

1. I asked him how old he thought I was. He said sixty, although he knew I wasn't that old. Do I look that bad? I asked. Worse, he said. And you think you're in better shape? I said. How come you're shaking, then? Are you cold? Have you gone crazy? And why are you telling me about Commissioner Damian Valle anyway? Is he still the commissioner? Is he still the same? The old guy said Valle had changed a bit, but he was still a prize son of a bitch. Is he still the commissioner? He might as well be, he said. If he wants to do you harm, he will, even if he's retired or dying in a hospital. I thought for a few minutes and then asked him again why he was shaking. I'm cold, he said (the liar), and my teeth hurt. I don't want to hear any more about Don Damian, I said. Do you think I'm friends with that pig? Do you think I associate with thugs? No, he said. Well I don't want to hear any more about him. **2.** He reflected for a while. What about, I really don't know. Then he gave me a crust of bread. It was hard and I said if he ate food like that it wasn't surprising his teeth hurt. We eat better in the asylum, I said, and that's saying something. Get out of here, Vicente, said the old guy. Does anyone know you're here? Well, good for you. Make yourself scarce before they realize. Don't say hello to anyone. Keep your eyes on the ground and get out of here as fast as you can. **3.** But I didn't leave right away. I squatted down in front of him and tried to remember the good times. My mind was blank. It felt like something was burning in my head. The old guy pulled his blanket tighter around him and moved his jaws as if he was chewing, but there was nothing in his mouth. I remembered the years in the asylum: the injections, the hosing down, the ropes they used for tying us up at night, many of us anyway. I saw those funny beds again, the ones with a clever system of pulleys that can be used to hoist them into an upright position. It took me five years to work out what they were for. The patients called them American beds. **4.** Can a human being who is used to sleeping horizontally fall asleep in an upright position? Yes. It's difficult at first. But if the person is properly tied, it's possible. That's what the American beds were for, sleeping vertically as well as horizontally. Not, as I originally thought, to punish the patients, but to prevent them from choking on their own vomit and dying. **5.** Naturally, there were patients who spoke to the American beds. They addressed them politely. They confided in them. Some patients were also afraid of them. Some claimed to have been winked at by a certain bed. One patient said that another bed had raped him. A bed fucked you up the ass? You've really lost it, pal! The American beds were said to walk along the corridors at night, straight and tall, and gather to chat in the refectory—they spoke English—and all of them attended those meetings, the beds that were empty and the ones that weren't, and naturally these stories were told by the patients who for one reason or another happened to be tied to the beds on meeting nights. **6.** Otherwise, life in the asylum was very quiet. Shouts could be heard coming from certain restricted areas. But no one approached those areas or opened the door or put their ear to the keyhole. The house was quiet, and the park—tended by gardeners who were crazy too and not allowed to leave, but not as crazy as the others—was quiet as well, and the road you could see through the pines and the poplars was quiet, and even our thoughts, as they occurred to us, were enveloped in a frightening silence. **7.** In certain respects, the living was easy. Sometimes we'd look at each other and feel privileged. We're crazy, we're innocent. The only thing that spoiled that feeling was anticipation, when there was something to anticipate. But most of the patients had a remedy for that: ass-fucking the weaker ones or getting ass-fucked. Did I do that? we used to say. Did I really do that? And then we'd smile and change the subject. The doctors, the lofty physicians, had no idea, and as long as we didn't bother the nurses and the aides, they turned a blind eye. We did get carried away a few times. Man is an animal. **8.** That's what I used to think sometimes. The thought formed in the center of my brain. And I concentrated on that thought until my mind went blank. Sometimes, at the beginning, I could hear something like tangling cables. Electrical cables or snakes. But as a rule, especially as those scenes receded into the past, my mind would go blank: no noises, no images, no words, no breakwaters of words. **9.** Anyway, I've never assumed that I'm smarter than anybody else. I've never been an intellectual show-off. If I'd been to school, I'd be a lawyer or a judge now. Or the inventor of a new, improved American bed! I have words, that much I humbly admit. But I don't make a big deal about it. And just as I have words, I have silence. You're as silent as a cat, the old guy told me when I was still a kid, though he was old already then. **10.** I wasn't born here. According to the old guy, I was born in Zaragoza and my mother had no choice but to come and live in this city. One city or another, it makes no difference to me. If I hadn't been poor, I would have been able to study here. It doesn't matter! I learned to read. That's enough! Best not to dwell on that subject. I could have got married here too. I met a girl who was called, I forget, she had a typical girl's name, and at one point I could have married her. Then I met another girl, older than me, a foreigner like me, from somewhere in the south, Andalusia or Murcia, a slut who was always in a bad mood. I could have started a family with her too, made a home, but I was destined for other things, and so was the slut. **11.** Sometimes I found the city stifling. Too small. I felt as if I were locked in a crossword puzzle. **12.** Around that time I made up my mind to start begging at church doors. I would arrive at ten and take up my position on the cathedral steps or go to the church of San Jeremías, in the Calle José Antonio, or the church of Santa Barbara, which was my favorite, in the Calle Salamanca, and sometimes, before settling down on the steps of Santa Barbara to begin my day's work, I would go to the ten o'clock mass and pray with all my might—it was like laughing silently, laughing, laughing, happy to be alive, and the more I prayed, the more I laughed—that was my way of opening myself to divine penetration, and my laughter was not a sign of disrespect or the laughter of an unbeliever: on the contrary, it was the clamorous laughter of a lamb trembling before its Creator. **13.** After that, I would go to Confession, recount my mishaps and misfortunes, take Communion, and finally, before returning to the steps, I would stop for a few moments in front of the picture of St. Barbara. Why was she always depicted with a peacock and a tower? A peacock and a tower. What did it mean? **14.** One afternoon I asked the priest. Why are you interested in such things? he asked me in turn. I don't know, Father, curiosity, I replied. You know it's a bad habit, don't you, curiosity? he said. I know, Father, but my curiosity is pure, I always pray to St. Barbara. That's good, my son, said the priest, St. Barbara is kind to the poor, you keep praying to her. But I want to know about the peacock and the tower, I said. The peacock, said the priest, is the symbol of immortality. As for the tower, did you notice it has three windows? The windows are there to illustrate the saint's words; she said that light poured into her cell and her soul through the windows of the Father, the Son, and the Holy Spirit. Do you understand? **15.** I didn't get an education, Father, but I have common sense and I can work things out, I replied. **16.** Then I went to take my place, the place that was rightfully mine, and I begged until the church doors were closed. I always kept one coin in the palm of my hand. The others in my pocket. And I endured hunger, while people ate bread and pieces of sausage or cheese in front of me. I thought. I thought and studied without moving from those steps. **17.** And so I learned that the father of St. Barbara, a powerful man named Dioscurus, shut her up in a tower, imprisoned her because she was being pursued by suitors. And I learned that, before entering that tower, St. Barbara baptized herself with water from a tank or a trough or a pond in which farmers stored rainwater. And I learned that she escaped from the tower, the tower with three windows to let the light in, but was arrested and brought before a judge. And the judge condemned her to death. **18.** All the teachings of the priests are cold. Cold soup. Cold tea. Blankets that don't keep you warm in the depths of winter. **19.** Get out of here, Vicente, said the old guy, his jaws working all the while. As if he was chewing sunflower seeds. Get some clothes to make you blend in and go, before the commissioner finds out. **20.** I put my hand in my pocket and counted the coins. It had begun to snow. I said goodbye to the old guy and went out into the street. **21.** I walked aimlessly. With no destination. Standing in the Calle Corona, I looked at the Church of Santa Barbara. I prayed a bit. St. Barbara, have pity on me, I said. My left arm had gone to sleep. I was hungry. I wanted to die. But not for good. Maybe I just wanted to sleep. My teeth were chattering. St. Barbara, have pity on your servant. **22.** When they decapitated her, I mean when they cut St. Barbara's head off, her executioners were struck by a bolt of lightning. And what about the judge who sentenced her? And her father who locked her up? The lightning struck, but first there was a clap of thunder. Or the other way around. Great. My God, my God, my God. **23.** I didn't go any closer. I was happy to look at the church from a distance and then I walked on, heading for a bar where in my day you used to be able to get a cheap meal. I couldn't find it. I went into a bakery and got a baguette. Then I jumped a wall and ate it, out of sight of prying eyes. I know it's forbidden to jump over walls and eat in abandoned gardens or derelict houses, because it isn't safe. A beam could fall on you, Commissioner Damian Valle told me. Also, it's private property. It might be a shit-heap, crawling with spiders and rats, but it will go on being private property until the end of time. And a beam could fall on your head and destroy that exceptional skull of yours, said Commissioner Damian Valle. **24.** When I'd finished eating, I jumped back over the wall into the street. Suddenly I felt sad. I don't know if it was the snow or what. Recently, eating gets me down. I'm not sad when I'm actually eating, but afterward, sitting on a brick, watching snowflakes fall into the abandoned garden—I don't know. Despair and anguish. So I slapped my legs and got walking. The streets started to empty out. I spent some time looking in store windows. But I was pretending. What I was really doing was looking for my reflection in each pane of glass. Then the windows came to an end and there were only stairways. I hung my head and climbed. A street. Then the parish church of the Conception. Then the church of San Bernardo. Then the walls and, after that, the fort. There wasn't a soul to be seen. I was on Cerro del Moro. I remembered the old man's words: Go, go, don't let them catch you again, you poor bastard. All the bad things I did. St. Barbara, have pity on me, have pity on your poor son. I remembered there was a woman who lived in one of those alleys. I decided to visit her and ask for a bowl of soup, an old sweater she didn't need anymore, and a bit of money to buy a train ticket. Where did that woman live? The alleys kept getting narrower. I saw a big door and knocked. No one answered. I pushed the door open and walked in: a patio. Someone had forgotten to take in the washing and now the snow was falling on those yellowish clothes. I made my way through the shirts and underpants to a door with a bronze knocker that looked like a handle. I stroked the knocker, but I didn't knock. I pushed the door open. Outside, night was falling hurriedly. My mind was blank. The snowflakes made a sizzling sound. I kept going. I couldn't remember that corridor, I couldn't remember the name of the woman—she was a slut, but kindhearted; she did wrong but she felt bad about it—I couldn't remember that darkness, that windowless tower. But then I saw a door ajar and slipped through the opening. I'd come to a kind of granary, with sacks piled up to the roof. There was a bed in one corner. I saw a child stretched out on the bed. He was naked and shivering. I took the knife out of my pocket. I saw a friar sitting at a table. His face was covered by a hood; he was leaning forward, intently reading a missal. Why was the child naked? Wasn't there even a blanket in that room? Why was the friar reading his missal instead of kneeling down and asking for forgiveness. Everything goes haywire at some point. The friar looked at me, said something; I replied. Don't come near me, I said. Then I stabbed him with the knife. Both of us groaned for a while until he fell silent. But I had to be sure, so I stabbed him again. Then I killed the child. Quickly, for God's sake! Then I sat down on the bed and shivered for a while. Enough. I had to go. My clothes were spattered with blood. I looked through the friar's pockets and found some money. There were some sweet potatoes on the table. I ate one. Good and sweet. While I was eating the sweet potato, I opened a closet. Sacks of onions and potatoes. But there was also a clean habit on a hanger. I got undressed. It was so cold. After checking each pocket, so as not to leave any incriminating evidence, I put my clothes and my shoes in a bag, and tied it to my belt. Fuck you, Damian Valle. That was when I realized I was leaving my footprints all around the room. The soles of my feet were covered with blood. While continuing to move around, I carefully examined the prints. Suddenly I felt like laughing. They were dance steps. The footprints of St. Vitus. Footprints leading nowhere. But I knew where to go. **25.** Everything was dark, except for the snow. I started going down Cerro del Moro. **26.** I was barefoot and it was cold. My feet sank into the snow, and with every step I took, some blood came off my skin. When I'd gone a few yards I realized that someone was following me. A policeman? I didn't care. They rule the earth, but right then, as I walked through the luminous snow, I knew that I was in charge. **27.** I left Cerro del Moro behind. On the level ground the snow was deeper still; I crossed a bridge, hanging my head.

Out of the corner of my eye, I glimpsed the shadow of an equestrian statue. My pursuer was a fat, ugly adolescent. Who was I? That didn't matter at all. **28.** As I walked, I said goodbye to everything I saw. It was poignant. I quickened my pace to warm myself up. I crossed the bridge, and it was as if I had passed through a time tunnel. **29.** I could have killed the boy, made him follow me down an alley and stuck it to him till he croaked. But why bother? He was bound to be some whore's kid from Cerro del Moro; he'd never talk. **30.** I washed my old shoes in the bathroom at the station, I wet them and scrubbed away the bloodstains. My feet had gone to sleep. Wake up. Then I bought a ticket for the next train. Whichever, I didn't care where it was going.

LITERATURE + ILLNESS = ILLNESS

for my friend the hepatologist Dr. Victor Vargas

ILLNESS AND PUBLIC SPEAKING

No one should be surprised if the speaker loses his thread. Let us imagine the following scenario. The speaker is going to speak about illness. Ten people spread themselves around the auditorium. The buzz of anticipation in the air is worthy of a better reward. The talk is scheduled to begin at seven in the evening or eight at night. No one in the audience has had dinner. By seven (or eight, or nine), they are all present and seated, with their cell phones switched off. It's a pleasure to speak to such a well-mannered group of people. But the speaker fails to appear, and finally one of the organizers of the event announces that he will not be coming because, at the last minute, he has fallen gravely ill.

ILLNESS AND FREEDOM

Writing about illness, especially if one is gravely ill, can be torture. Writing about illness if one is not only gravely ill but also a hypochondriac is an act of masochism or desperation. But it can also be a liberating act. It's tempting—I know it's an evil temptation—but all the same it *is* tempting to exercise the tyranny of the ill for a few minutes, like those little old ladies you meet in hospital waiting rooms, who launch into an explanation of the clinical or medical or pharmacological aspects of their life, instead of explaining the political or sexual or work-related aspects. Little old ladies who give the impression that they have transcended good and evil, and look for all the world like they know their Nietzsche, and not just Nietzsche, but Kant and Hegel and Schelling too, not to mention their closest philosophical relative: Ortega y Gasset. They could be his sisters, or rather his cronies, although actually they're more like the philosopher's clones. The resemblance is so striking that sometimes (as I reach the limits of my desperation) it occurs to me that Ortega y Gasset's paradise, or his hell—depending on the gaze but above all the sensibility of the observer—is to be found in hospital waiting rooms: a paradise in which thousands of duplicates of Ortega y Gasset live out the various episodes of our lives. But I mustn't wander too far from what I really wanted to talk about, which, in fact, was freedom, a kind of liberation: writing badly, speaking badly, holding forth about plate tectonics in the middle of a reptiles' dinner party—it's so liberating and so richly deserved—offering myself up to the compassion of strangers and then dishing out insults at random, spitting as I talk, passing out indiscriminately, becoming a nightmare for the friends I don't deserve, *milking a cow and pouring the milk over its head*, as Nicanor Parra says in a magnificent and mysterious line.

ILLNESS AND HEIGHT

But let's if not get to the point at least approach it briefly, where it lies like a seed deposited by the wind or a pure chance bang in the middle of a vast bare tabletop. Not long ago, as I was leaving the consulting rooms of my specialist Victor Vargas, among the patients waiting to go in I found a woman waiting for me to come out. She was a small woman, by which I mean short; her head barely came up to my chest—the top of it would have been about an inch above my nipples—even though, as I soon realized, she was wearing spectacularly high heels. Needless to say, the consultation had not been reassuring, at all; the news my doctor had for me was unequivocally bad. I felt—I don't know—not exactly dizzy, which would have been understandable after all, but more as if everyone else had been stricken with dizziness, while I was the only one keeping reasonably calm and standing up straight, more or less. I had the impression that they were crawling on all fours, while I was upright or seated with my legs crossed, which for all intents and purposes is as good as standing or walking or maintaining a vertical position. I wouldn't, however, go so far as to say that I felt well, because it's one thing to remain upright while everyone else is on their hands and knees, and another thing entirely to watch, with a feeling I shall, for want of a better word, call *tenderness* or curiosity or morbid curiosity, while those around you are suddenly reduced, one and all, to crawling. Tenderness, melancholy, nostalgia: feelings befitting the sentimental lover, but hardly appropriate in the outpatients' ward of a Barcelona hospital. Of course, had that hospital been a mental asylum, such a vision would not have disturbed me at all, since from a tender age I have been familiar with—though never obeyed—the proverbial injunction, When in Rome, do as the Romans do, and the best way to behave in an asylum, apart from maintaining a dignified silence, is to crawl or observe the crawling of one's partners in misfortune. But I wasn't in an asylum; I was in one of the best public hospitals in Barcelona, a hospital that I know well, because I've been a patient there five or six times, and until that occasion I had never seen anyone on all fours, although I had seen some patients turn canary yellow, and others suddenly stop breathing—they were dying, which is not unusual in such a place—but crawling, I'd never seen anyone do that, which made me think that the doctor's news must have been much worse than I had initially realized, in other words, I was in *seriously* bad condition. And when I came out of the consulting rooms and saw everyone crawling, this sense of my own illness intensified, and I was about to succumb to fear and start crawling too. But I didn't, because of that little woman: she stepped forward and said her name, Dr. X, and then pronounced the name of my specialist, my dear Dr. Vargas—my relationship with him is like the marriage of a Greek shipping magnate who loves his wife but prefers to see her as rarely as he can—and Dr. X went on to say that she knew about my illness or the progress of my illness and that she would like me to participate in a study she was conducting. I asked her politely about the nature of the study. Her reply was vague. She explained that it would only take half an hour of my time, if that; she had a series of tests for me. I don't know why, but I ended up saying yes, and then she led me away from the consulting rooms to an elevator of impressive proportions, in which there was a gurney, with no one to push it, and no one on it, of course, a gurney that lived in the elevator, going up and down, like a normal-size girl alongside—or inside—her oversize boyfriend. It really was very large, that elevator, large enough to accommodate not just one gurney but two, plus a wheelchair, all with their respective occupants, and the strangest thing was that we were alone in there, the tiny doctor and myself, and at that point, having calmed down or become more excited, I'm not sure which, I realized that the tiny doctor was not at all bad-looking. No sooner had I come to that realization than I found myself wondering what would happen if I suggested that we make love in the elevator, since we had a bed at our disposal. And then, inevitably, I remembered Susan Sarandon, dressed up as a nun, asking Sean Penn how he could think about fucking when he had only a few days left to live. In a censorious tone of voice, of course. And, unsurprisingly, I've forgotten the name of the film, but it was a good film, I think it was directed by Tim Robbins, who's a good actor and maybe a good director too, but he's never been on death row. When people are about to die, all they want to do is fuck. People in jails and hospitals, all they want to do is fuck. The helpless, the impotent, the castrated, all they want to do is fuck. The seriously injured, the suicidal, the impenitent disciples of Heidegger. Even Wittgenstein, the greatest philosopher of the twentieth century, all he wanted to do was fuck. Even the dead, I read somewhere, all they want to do is fuck. Sad to say and hard to admit, but that's the way it is.

ILLNESS AND DIONYSUS

To tell the truth, the honest truth, cross my heart and hope to die, it's something I find very hard to admit. That seminal explosion, those cumulus and cirrus clouds that blanket our imaginary geography are enough to sadden anyone. Fucking when you don't have the strength to fuck can be beautiful, even epic. Then it turns into a nightmare. But what can you do? That's how it is. Consider, for instance, a Mexican jail. A new prisoner arrives. Not what you'd call handsome: squat, greasy, potbellied, cross-eyed, malevolent, and smelly into the bargain. Before long, this guy, whose shadow creeps over the prison walls or the walls of the corridors at an exasperating, slug-like pace, becomes the lover of another guy, who is just as ugly, but stronger. It's not a long, drawn-out romance, proceeding by tentative steps and hesitations. It's not a case of elective affinity, as Goethe understood it. It's love at first sight; primitive, if you like, but their objective is not so different from that of many normal couples or couples we consider to be normal. They are sweethearts. Their flirting and their swooning are like X-ray images. They fuck every night. Sometimes they hit each other. Sometimes they tell the stories of their lives, as if they were friends, but they're not really friends, they're lovers. And on Sundays, their respective wives, who are every bit as ugly as they are, come to visit. Obviously, neither of these men is what we would normally call a homosexual. If someone called them homosexuals to their faces, they'd probably get so angry and be so offended, they'd brutally rape the offender, then kill him. That's how it is. Victor Hugo, who, according to Daudet, was capable of eating a whole orange in one mouthful—a supreme test of good health, according to Daudet, and a sign of pig-like manners, according to my wife—set down the following reflection in *Les Misérables*: sinister people, malicious people know a sinister and malicious happiness. Or that's what I seem to remember, because *Les Misérables* is a book I read in Mexico many years ago and left behind in Mexico when I left Mexico for good, and I'm not planning to buy it or reread it, because there's no point reading, much less rereading, books that have been made into movies, and I think *Les Misérables* has even been turned into a musical. Anyway, the malicious people in question, with their malicious happiness, are the horrible family who adopt Cosette when she is a little girl, and not only are they the perfect incarnations of evil and a certain petit bourgeois meanness or rather the meanness of those who aspire to join the petit bourgeoisie, they are also, at this point in history, thanks to technological progress, emblematic of the middle class in its entirety, or almost, be it left- or right-wing, educated or illiterate, corrupt or apparently upstanding: healthy individuals, busily maintaining their good health; they may be less violent, less courageous, more prudent and more discreet, but basically they're just the same as the two Mexican gunmen living out their idyll in the confines of a penitentiary. There's no stopping Dionysus. He has infiltrated the churches and the NGOs, the governments and the royal families, the offices and the shantytowns. Dionysus is to blame for everything. Dionysus rules. And his antagonist or counterpart is not even Apollo but Mr. Uppity or Mrs. Toplofty, Mr. Prissy or Mrs. Lonely Neuron—bodyguards who are ready to cross over to the enemy camp at the first suspicious bang.

ILLNESS AND APOLLO

Where has that faggot Apollo got to? Apollo is ill, seriously ill.

ILLNESS AND FRENCH POETRY

As the French are well aware, the finest poetry of the nineteenth century was written in France, and in some sense the pages and the lines of that poetry prefigured the major and still unresolved problems that Europe and Western culture were to face in the twentieth century. A short list of the key themes would include revolution, death, boredom, and escape. That great poetry is the work of a handful of poets, and its point of departure is not Lamartine, or Hugo or Nerval, but Baudelaire. Let's say that it begins with Baudelaire, reaches its highest volatility with Lautréamont and Rimbaud and comes to an end with Mallarmé. Of course there are other remarkable poets, like Corbière or Verlaine, and others of considerable talent, like Laforgue or Catulle Mendès or Charles Cros, and even a few who are not entirely insignificant, like Banville. But, really, with Baudelaire, Lautréamont, Rimbaud, and Mallarmé, there's plenty to be going on with. Let's begin with the last of the four. I don't mean the youngest, but the last one to die, Mallarmé, who missed out on the twentieth century by two years. He wrote in *Brise marine*:

> The flesh is sad—and I've read every book.
> O to escape—to get away. Birds look
> as though they're drunk for unknown spray and skies.
> No ancient gardens mirrored in the eyes,
> nothing can hold this heart steeped in the sea —
> not my lamp's desolate luminosity
> nor the blank paper guarded by its white
> nor the young wife feeding her child, O night!
> I'm off! You steamer with your swaying helm,
> raise anchor for some more exotic realm!
> Ennui, crushed down by cruel hopes, still relies
> on handkerchief's definitive goodbyes!
> Is this the kind of squall-inviting mast
> the storm winds buckle above shipwrecks cast
> away—no mast, no islets flourishing? . . .
> Still, my soul, listen to the sailors sing!

A charming poem. Although Nabokov would have advised the translators, E. H. and A. M. Blackmore, to abandon the rhyme scheme, to use free verse, to produce a deliberately ugly version, and if he'd known Alfonso Reyes, who translated the poem into Spanish, with rhymes, he'd have given him the same advice. Now Reyes might not mean a lot to Western culture as a whole, but he does (or should) mean a great deal to that part of Western culture that is Latin America. What did Mallarmé mean when he said that the flesh was sad and that he'd read all the books? That he'd had his fill of reading and of fucking? That beyond a certain point, every book we read and every act of carnal knowledge is a repetition? And after that there is only travel? That fucking and reading are boring in the end, and that travel is the only way out? I think Mallarmé is talking about illness, about the battle between illness and health: two totalitarian states, or powers if you prefer. I think he's talking about illness tricked out in the rags of boredom. And yet he presents an image of illness that has a certain originality; he speaks of illness as *resignation*, resignation to living, or to whatever. In other words, he's talking about defeat. And in order to counter that defeat, he vainly invokes sex and reading, which, I suspect, in Mallarmé's case—to his greater glory and the bemusement of his good wife—were interchangeable, because how else could anyone in their right mind say that the flesh is sad, period, in that emphatic way? How could anyone declare that the flesh is *essentially* sad, that *la petite mort*, which doesn't even last a minute, casts a pall over all lovemaking, which, it is widely known, can last for hours and hours, and go on interminably? If the line had been written by a Spanish poet like Campoamor, it might have meant something like that, but such a reading is quite at odds with the work and life of Mallarmé, which are indissolubly linked, except in this poem, this encoded manifesto, which Paul Gauguin, and he alone, followed to the letter (as far as we know, Mallarmé himself never listened to the sailors singing, or if he did, it certainly wasn't on board a ship bound for an unknown destination). And the claim to have read all the books makes even less sense, because although books themselves may come to an end, no one ever finishes reading them all, and Mallarmé was well aware of that. Books are finite, sexual encounters are finite, but the desire to read and to fuck is infinite; it surpasses our own deaths, our fears, our hopes for peace. And what is left for Mallarmé, in this famous poem, when the desire to read and the desire to fuck, so he says, are all used up? Well, what is left is travel, the desire to go traveling. And maybe that's the key to the crime. Because if Mallarmé had concluded that the only thing left to do was pray or cry or go crazy, maybe he'd have come up with the perfect alibi. But no, what Mallarmé says is that the only thing left to do is travel—which is like saying "to sail is necessary, to live is not necessary," a sentence I used to be able to quote in Latin, but that's just one of the many things I've forgotten with the help of my liver's traveling toxins—in other words he sides with the bare-chested traveler, with Freedom (who's bare-chested too), with the simple existence of the sailor and the explorer, which isn't so simple when you get right down to it: an affirmation of life, but also a constant game with death, and the first rung on the ladder, the first step in a certain kind of poetic apprenticeship. The second step is sex, and the third, books. Which means that the Mallarmean choice is paradoxical or regressive, a starting over. And at this point, before we return to the elevator, I can't help recalling a poem by Baudelaire, the father of them all, in which he speaks of travel, the voyage, the naïve enthusiasm of setting out, and the bitterness that every voyage bequeaths to the voyager when all is said and done, and it occurs to me that perhaps Mallarmé's sonnet is a reply to Baudelaire's poem, one of the most terrible poems I have read, an *ill poem*, a poem that offers no way out, but perhaps the most clear-eyed poem of the entire nineteenth century.

ILLNESS AND TRAVEL

Traveling makes you ill. In the old days, doctors used to recommend travel, especially for patients suffering from nervous illnesses. The patients, who were generally wealthy, complied and set off on long trips that lasted months and sometimes years. Poor people who had nervous illnesses didn't get to travel. Some, presumably, went crazy. But the traveling patients also went crazy, or, worse still, acquired new illnesses as they moved from one city or climate or culinary culture to another. Really, it's healthier not to travel; it's healthier not to budge and never leave home, warmly wrapped up in winter, only removing your scarf in summertime; it's healthier not to open your mouth or blink; it's healthier not to breathe. But the fact is, we breathe and travel. Myself, for example, I began traveling very young, at the age of seven or eight. First in my father's truck, on lonely Chilean highways that had a post-nuclear feel to them and made my hair bristle, then in trains and buses, until at the age of fifteen, I boarded a plane for the first time and went to live in Mexico. From that moment on, I was constantly traveling. Consequence: multiple illnesses. In childhood: major headaches, which made my parents wonder if I had a nervous illness, and whether it might be advisable for me to undertake, as soon as possible, a long therapeutic voyage. In adolescence: insomnia and problems of a sexual nature. As a young man: the loss of my teeth, which I left here and there on my way from country to country, like Hansel and Gretel's breadcrumbs; a bad diet, which gave me heartburn and then gastritis; excessive reading, which weakened my eyes, so I had to wear glasses; calluses on my feet from long, aimless walks; and an endless string of lingering colds and flus. I was poor, lived rough, and thought myself lucky because, after all, I was free of life-threatening illnesses. My sex life was immoderate but I never caught a venereal disease. I read immoderately, but I never wanted to be a successful author. I even regarded the loss of my teeth as a kind of homage to Gary Snyder, whose life of Zen wandering had led him to neglect dental care. But it all catches up with you. Children. Books. Illness. The voyage comes to an end.

ILLNESS AND DEAD ENDS

Baudelaire's poem is called "The Voyage." It is a long and delirious poem, possessed of the delirium that results from extreme lucidity, and this is not the moment to read it all the way through. Here are the first lines in Richard Howard's translation:

> The child enthralled by lithographs and maps
> can satisfy his hunger for the world

The poem, then, begins with a child. *Naturally* the poem of adventure and horror begins with the pure gaze of a child. Then it goes on:

> One morning we set out. Our heart is full,
> our mind ablaze with rancor and disgust,
> we yield it all to the rhythm of the waves,
> our infinite self awash on the finite sea:
>
> some are escaping from their country's shame,
> some from the horror of life at home, and some
> —astrologers blinded by a woman's stare—
> are fugitives from Circe's tyranny;
> rather than be turned to swine they drug
> themselves on wind and sea and glowing skies;
> rain and snow and incinerating suns
> gradually erase her kisses' scars.
>
> But only those who leave for leaving's sake
> are travelers; hearts tugging like balloons,
> they never balk at what they call their fate
> and, not knowing why, keep muttering "away" . . .

In a way, the voyage undertaken by the crew in Baudelaire's poem is similar to the voyage of a convict ship. I shall set off, I shall venture into unknown territory, and see what I find, see what happens. But first I shall give up everything. Or to put it another way: genuine travel requires travelers who have nothing to lose. The voyage, this long and hazardous nineteenth-century voyage, resembles the patient's voyage on a gurney, from his room to the operating theater, where masked men and women await him, like bandits from the sect of the Hashishin. It's true that the early stages of the voyage are not devoid of paradisiacal visions, which owe more to the travelers' desires or cultural background than to reality:

> Awesome travelers! What noble chronicles
> we read in your unfathomable eyes!
> Open the sea-chests of your memories

The poem also says: Tell us what you've seen! And the traveler, or the ghost that represents the traveler and his companions, replies by listing the circles of Hell. Baudelaire's traveler clearly isn't saying that the flesh is sad or that he has read all the books, although he just as clearly knows that entropy's gem and trophy, the flesh, is more than merely sad, and that once a single book has been read, all the others have been read as well. Baudelaire's traveler has a full heart and a mind ablaze with rancor and disgust, which means that he's probably a radical, modern traveler, although of course he's someone who, understandably, wants to come through; he wants to *see*, but he also wants to come through it alive. The voyage, as it unfolds in the poem, is like a ship or an unruly caravan heading straight for the abyss, but the traveler, to judge from his disgust, desperation, and scorn, wants to come through it alive. And what he finds in the end, like Ulysses or the patient traveling on his gurney who confuses the ceiling with the abyss, is his own image:

> It is a bitter truth our travels teach!
> Tiny and monotonous, the world
> has shown—will always show us—what we are:
> oases of fear in the wasteland of ennui!

In that line alone there is more than enough. In the middle of a desert of ennui, an oasis of fear, or horror. There is no more lucid diagnosis of the illness of modern humanity. To break out of ennui, to escape from boredom, all we have at our disposal—and it's not even automatically at our disposal, again we have to make an effort—is horror, in other words, evil. Either we live like zombies, like slaves fed on soma, or we become slave drivers, malignant individuals, like that guy who, after killing his wife and three children, said, as the sweat poured off him, that he felt strange, possessed by something he'd never known: freedom, and then he said that the victims had deserved it, although a few hours later, when he'd calmed down a bit, he also said that no one deserved to die so horribly, and added that he'd probably gone crazy and told the police not to listen to him. An oasis is always an oasis, especially if you come to it from a desert of boredom. In an oasis you can drink, eat, tend to your wounds, and rest, but if it's an oasis of horror, if that's the only sort there is, the traveler will be able to confirm, and this time irrefutably, that the flesh is sad, that a day comes when all the books have indeed been read, and that travel is the pursuit of a mirage. All the indications are that every oasis in existence has either attained or is drifting toward the condition of horror.

ILLNESS AND THE DOCUMENTARY

One of the most vivid images of illness I can recall is of a guy whose name I've forgotten, a New York artist who worked in the space between begging and the avant-garde, between the adepts of fist-fucking and the modern-day mendicants. One night, years ago, very late, when the TV audience had dwindled to me, I saw him in a documentary. He was an extreme masochist, and extracted the raw materials of his art from his proclivity or fate or incurable vice. Half actor, half painter. As I remember, he wasn't very tall and he was going bald. He filmed his experiments: scenes or dramatizations of pain. Pain that grew more and more intense, and sometimes brought the artist to the brink of death. One day, after a routine visit to the hospital, they tell him he has a fatal illness. At first he is surprised. But the surprise doesn't last long. Almost straightaway, the guy begins to film his final performance, which, as opposed to the earlier ones, turns out to be admirably restrained, at least at the start. He seems calm and, above all, subdued, as if he had ceased to believe in the effectiveness of wild gestures and overacting. We see him, for example, on a bicycle, pedaling along a kind of seaside boulevard—it must be Coney Island—then sitting on a breakwater, reminiscing about unrelated scenes from his childhood and adolescence while he looks at the ocean and occasionally throws a sidelong glance at the camera. His voice and expression are neither cold nor warm. He doesn't sound like an alien, or a man desperately hiding under his bed with his eyes shut tight. Perhaps he has the voice, and the expression, of a blind man, but if so, it is clearly the voice of a blind man addressing himself to the blind. I wouldn't say that he has serenely accepted his fate or resolved to resist it with all his strength, what I would say is that he is a man who is utterly indifferent to his fate. The final scenes take place in the hospital. The guy knows he won't be getting out of there alive; he knows that death is the only thing left, but he still looks at the camera, whose function is to document this final performance. And only at this point does the sleepless viewer realize that there are in fact two cameras, and two films: the documentary that he is watching on television, a French or German production, and the documentary recording the performance, which will follow the artist whose name I've forgotten or never knew right up to the moment of his death, the documentary that he is directing, with an iron hand or an iron gaze, from his procrustean bed. That's how it is. A voice, the voice of the French or German narrator, says goodbye to the New Yorker, and then, when the screen has faded to black, pronounces the date of his death, a few weeks later. The pain artist's documentary, however, follows the dying step by step, but we don't see that, we can only imagine it, or let the image fade to black and read the clinical date of his death, because if we watched, if we saw, it would be unbearable.

ILLNESS AND POETRY

Between the vast deserts of boredom and the not-so-scarce oases of horror, there is, however, a third option, or perhaps a delusion, which Baudelaire indicates in the following lines:

> Once we have burned our brains out, we can plunge
> to Hell or Heaven—any abyss will do—
> deep in the Unknown to find the *new*!

That final line, deep in the Unknown to find the new, is art's paltry flag pitting itself against the horror that adds to horror without making a substantial difference, just as one infinity added to another produces an infinite sum. A losing battle from the start, like all the battles poets fight. This is something that Lautréamont seems to contradict, because his voyage takes him from the periphery to the metropolis, and his way of traveling and seeing remains cloaked in the most impenetrable mystery, so that we can't tell if we're dealing with a militant nihilist or an outrageous optimist or the secret mastermind of the imminent Commune; and it's something that Rimbaud clearly understood, since he plunged with equal fervor into reading, sex, and travel, only to discover and accept, with a diamond-like lucidity, that writing doesn't matter at all (writing is obviously the same as reading, and sometimes it's quite similar to traveling, and it can even, on special occasions, resemble sex, but all that, Rimbaud tells us, is a mirage: there is only the desert and from time to time the remote, degrading lights of an oasis). And then along comes Mallarmé, the least innocent of all the great poets, who says that we must travel, we must set off traveling again. At this point, even the most naïve reader has to wonder: What's got into Mallarmé? Why is he so enthusiastic? Is he trying to sell us a trip or sending us to our deaths with our hands and feet tied? Is this an elaborate joke or simply a pattern of sounds? It would be utterly absurd to suppose that Mallarmé had not read Baudelaire. So what is he trying to do? The answer, I think, is perfectly simple. Mallarmé wants to start all over again, even though he knows that the voyage and the voyagers are doomed. In other words, for the author of *Igitur*, the illness afflicts not only our actions, but also language itself. But while we are looking for the antidote or the medicine to cure us, that is, the *new*, which can only be found by plunging deep into the Unknown, we have to go on exploring sex, books, and travel, although we know that they lead us to the abyss, which, as it happens, is the only place where the antidote can be found.

ILLNESS AND TESTS

And now it is time to return to that enormous elevator, the biggest I've ever seen, an elevator in which there was space enough for a shepherd to pen a smallish flock of sheep, or a farmer to stable two mad cows, or a nurse to fit two empty gurneys, and in which I was torn between asking the tiny doctor—almost as small as a Japanese doll—if she would make love with me, or at least give it a try, and (this was the likelier option) bursting into tears, like Alice in Wonderland, and flooding the elevator not with blood, as in Kubrick's *The Shining*, but with salt water. This was one of those situations in which good manners, which are never redundant, and rarely a hindrance, did in fact hinder me, and soon the Japanese doctor and I were shut in a cubicle, with a window from which you could see the back part of the hospital, doing some very odd tests, which seemed to me exactly like the tests you find on the puzzle page of the Sunday paper. I was careful to do them as well as I could, as if I wanted to prove to her that my specialist was mistaken—a futile enterprise, because however perfectly I did the tests, the little Japanese doctor remained impassive: not even a tiny smile of encouragement. Between tests, while she was getting the next one ready, we talked. I asked her about the chances of success with a liver transplant. Vely good, she said. What percent? I asked. Sixty percent, she said. Jesus, I said, that's not much. In politics it's absolute majolity, she said. One of the tests, maybe the simplest, made a big impression on me. It consisted of holding my hands out in a vertical position for a few seconds, that is, with the fingers pointing up, the palms facing her, and the backs to me. I asked her what the hell that test was about. Her reply was that at a more advanced stage of my illness, I wouldn't be able to hold my fingers in that position. They would, inevitably, curve toward her. I think I said: Christ almighty. Maybe I laughed. In any case, every day since then, wherever I happen to be, I take that test. I hold my hands out, palms facing away, and for a few seconds I examine my knuckles, my nails, the wrinkles that form on each phalange. The day when my fingers can't hold themselves up straight, I don't really know what I'll do, although I do know what I *won't* do. Mallarmé wrote that a roll of the dice will never abolish chance. And yet every day the dice have to be rolled, just as the vertical-fingers test has to be taken every day.

ILLNESS AND KAFKA

Elias Canetti, in his book on the twentieth century's greatest writer, says that Kafka understood that the dice had been rolled and that nothing could come between him and writing the day he spat blood for the first time. What do I mean when I say that nothing could come between him and his writing? To be honest, I don't really know. I guess I mean that Kafka understood that travel, sex, and books are paths that lead nowhere except to the loss of the self, and yet they must be followed and the self must be lost, in order to find it again, or to find something, whatever it may be—a book, an expression, a misplaced object—in order to find anything at all, a method, perhaps, and, with a bit of luck, the *new*, which has been there all along.

THE MYTHS OF CTHULHU

for Alan Pauls

These are dark times we live in, but let me begin with a buoyant declaration. Literature in Spanish is in excellent condition! Magnificent, superlative condition!

In fact, if it was any better I'd be worried.

But let's not get too carried away. It's good, but it's not going to give anyone a heart attack. There's nothing to suggest any kind of great leap forward.

According to a critic by the name of Conte, Pérez-Reverte is Spain's perfect novelist. I don't have a copy of the article in which he makes that claim, so I can't cite it exactly. As I recall, he said that Pérez-Reverte was the *most* perfect novelist in contemporary Spanish literature, as if it were possible to go on perfecting oneself after having achieved perfection. His principal quality, but I don't know if it was Conte who said this or the novelist Juan Marsé, is readability. A readability that makes him not only the most perfect novelist but also the most read. That is: the one who sells the most books.

But if we adopt that point of view, Spanish fiction's perfect novelist could just as well be Vázquez-Figueroa, who spends his spare time inventing desalination machines or desalination plants: contraptions that will soon be turning seawater into fresh water, suitable for irrigation, showers, and probably even for drinking. Vázquez-Figueroa might not be the *most* perfect, but he certainly is perfect in his way. He's readable. He's enjoyable. He sells a lot. His stories, like those of Pérez-Reverte, are full of adventures.

I really wish I had a copy of Conte's review. It's a pity I don't collect press clippings, like that character in Cela's *The Beehive*, who keeps an article that he wrote for a provincial newspaper, probably one of the Workers' Movement papers, in the pocket of his shabby jacket—a likable character, by the way; in the movie, he was played by José Sacristán, and that's how I always see him in my mind's eye, with that pale helpless face, the incongruous face of a beaten dog, carrying that crumpled clipping around in his pocket as he wanders over the impossible tablelands of Spain. At this point I hope you'll allow me to indulge in a pair of elucidatory digressions or sighs: José Sacristán, what a fine actor! His performances are so enjoyable, so readable. And Camilo José Cela, what an odd phenomenon! More and more he reminds me of a Chilean estate-holder or a Mexican rancher; his illegitimate children (as Latin Americans would politely say) or his bastards keep springing up like weeds: vulgar, reluctant, but tenacious and gruff, like candid lilacs out of the dead land, as the candid Eliot put it.

By attaching Cela's incredibly fat corpse to a horse, we could produce the new El Cid of Spanish letters, and we have!

Statement of principles:

In principle, I have nothing against clear, enjoyable writing. In practice, it depends.

It's always a good idea to state this principle when venturing into the world of literature: a sort of Club Med cunningly disguised as a swamp, a desert, a working-class suburb, or a novel-as-mirror reflecting itself.

Here's a rhetorical question that I'd like someone to answer for me: Why does Pérez-Reverte or Vázquez-Figueroa or any other bestselling author, for example Muñoz Molina or that young man who goes by the resonant name of de Prada, sell so much? Is it just because their books are enjoyable and easy to follow? Is it just because they tell stories that keep the reader in suspense? Won't anyone give me an answer? Where is the man who will dare to answer? It's all right, you can keep quiet. I hate to see people lose their friends. I'll answer the question myself. The answer is no. It's not just that. They sell and they are popular because their stories can be *understood.* That is, because the readers, who are never wrong—I don't mean as readers, obviously, but as consumers, of books in this case—understand their novels or stories perfectly. This is something that the critic Conte knows, or perhaps, given his youth, intuits. It's something that the novelist Marsé, who is old, has learned from experience. The public, the public, as García Lorca said to a hustler while they hid in an entrance hall, is never, never, never wrong. And why is the public never wrong? Because the public *understands*.

It is, of course, only reasonable to accept and indeed to demand that a novel should be clear and entertaining, since the novel, as an art form, is at best tenuously related to the great forces that shape public history and our private stories, namely science and television; nevertheless, when the rule of clarity and entertainment value is extended to serious nonfiction and philosophy, the results can be catastrophic, at least at first glance, although the idea, the ideal, remains compelling, a goal to be desired and aspired to in the longer term. "Weak thought," for example. Honestly, I have no idea what weak thought was or is supposed to be. Its promoter, I seem to remember, was a twentieth-century Italian philosopher. I never read any of his books or any book about him. One reason—this is a fact, not an excuse—is that I had no money to buy books. So I must have learned of his existence in the pages of some newspaper. That's how I discovered that there was such a thing as weak thought. The philosopher is probably still alive. But in the end he's immaterial. Maybe I completely misunderstood what he meant by weak thought. Probably. But what matters is the *title* of his book. Just as when we talk about *Don Quixote*, what we're usually referring to is not so much the book itself as the title and a couple of windmills. And when we talk about Kafka (may God forgive me), it's less about Kafka and the fire than a lady or a gentleman at a window. (This is known as encapsulation, an image retained and metabolized by the body, fixed in historical memory, the solidification of chance and fate.) The strength of weak thought—this intuition came to me in a fit of dizziness, brought on by hunger—sprang from the way it presented itself as a philosophical method for people unfamiliar with philosophical systems. Weak thought for the weak classes. With a bit of well-targeted marketing, a construction worker in Gerona, who has never sat down on the scaffolding, thirty yards above street level, with his copy of the *Tractatus Logico-Philosophicus*, or reread it while chewing through his *chope* roll, might be prompted to read the Italian philosopher instead or one of his disciples, whose clear, enjoyable, intelligible style is bound to go straight to his heart.

At that moment, in spite of the dizziness, I felt like Nietzsche when he had his Eternal Return epiphany. An inexorable succession of nanoseconds, each one blessed by eternity.

What is *chope*? What does a *chope* roll consist of? Is the bread rubbed with tomato and a few drops of olive oil, or is it just plain bread that is wrapped in aluminum foil, also known by its brand name as *albal*? And what does the *chope* consist of?

Mortadella cheese, maybe? Or a mixture of mortadella and boiled ham? Or salami and mortadella? Does it contain chorizo or sausage? And how did the foil come to have the brand name *albal*? Is it a family name, the name of Mr. Nemesio Albal? Or is it an allusion to *el alba*, the dawn, the bright dawn of lovers and workers who, before setting off for their daily labor, put a pound of bread and the corresponding ration of sliced *chope* into their lunch boxes?

Dawn with a slight metallic sheen. Bright dawn over the shithole. That was the title of a poem I wrote with Bruno Montané centuries ago. The other day I came across the title and the poem attributed to another poet. Honestly, honestly, what are these people thinking? The lengths they go to, tracking, poaching, harassing. And the worst thing is, it's an appalling title.

But let us return to weak thought, which goes down like a treat on the scaffolding. It's pleasant to read, you can't deny that. It isn't short on clarity either. And the socially weak or powerless understand the message perfectly. Hitler, to take another example, there was an essayist or philosopher—take your pick—who specialized in weak thought. He's always understandable! Self-help books are in fact books of practical philosophy, enjoyable down-to-earth philosophy that the woman and the man in the street can understand. That Spanish philosopher who analyzes and interprets the ups and downs of *Big Brother* is a readable and clear philosopher, although in his case the revelation came a couple of decades late. I can't recall his name for the moment, because, as many of you will have guessed, I am writing this speech on the fly a few days before delivering it. All I can remember is that the philosopher in question lived for many years in a Latin American country; I imagine him there feeling thoroughly sick of his tropical exile, and the mosquitoes, and the ghastly exuberance of the flowers of evil. Now the old philosopher lives in a Spanish city, somewhere north of Andalusia, enduring endless winters, muffled in a scarf and a woolen cap, watching the competitors in *Big Brother* and taking notes in a notebook with pages white and cold as snow.

For books about theology, there's no one to match Sánchez Dragó. For books about popular science, there's no one to match some guy whose name escapes me for the moment, a specialist in UFOs. For books about intertextuality, there's no one to match Lucía Etxebarría. For books about multiculturalism, there's no one to match Sánchez Dragó. For political books, there's no one to match Juan Goytisolo. For books about history and mythology, there's no one to match Sánchez Dragó. For a book about the ill-treatment of women today, there's no one to match that lovely talk show host Ana Rosa Quintana. For books about travel, there's no one to match Sánchez Dragó. I just love Sánchez Dragó. He doesn't look his age. I wonder if he dyes his hair with henna or ordinary dye from the hairdresser. Maybe his hair hasn't gone gray. And if he hasn't gone gray, how come he hasn't gone bald, which is what usually happens to men whose hair doesn't lose its original color?

•

And now for the question that has been tormenting me: Why hasn't Sánchez Dragó invited me to appear on his TV show? What is he waiting for? Does he want me to get down on my knees and grovel at his feet like a sinner before the burning bush? Is he waiting for my health to deteriorate even further? Or for me to get a recommendation from Pitita Ridruejo? Well, you watch out, Víctor Sánchez Dragó! There's a limit to my patience and I was a gangster in a former life! Don't say you weren't warned, Gregorio Sánchez Dragó!

Hear this. To the right-hand side of the routine signpost (coming—of course—from north-northwest), right where a bored skeleton yawns, you can already see Comala, the city of death. This speech is bound for that city, mounted on an ass, as all of us in our various more or less premeditated ways are bound for the city of Comala. But before we get there, I would like to relate a story told by Nicanor Parra, whom I would consider my master if I was worthy to be his disciple, which I'm not. One day, not so long ago, Nicanor Parra received an honorary doctorate from the University of Concepción. The honor might have been conferred by the University of Santa Barbara or Mulchén or Coigüe; I've been told that in the '90s all you needed to start up a private university in Chile was to have finished primary school and secured the use of a reasonable-size house; it's one of the boons of the free-market system. The University of Concepción, however, has a certain prestige; it's a big university and still a state-run institution as far as I know, and a tribute to Nicanor Parra was organized there and they gave him an honorary doctorate and invited him to conduct a master class. So Nicanor Parra turns up and the first thing he explains is that when he was a kid or a teenager, he went to that university—not to study, but to sell sandwiches (sometimes called *sánguches* in Chile), which the students used to wolf down between classes. Sometimes Nicanor Parra went there with his uncle, sometimes he went with his mother, and occasionally he went on his own, with a bag full of sandwiches, wrapped not in *albal* foil but in newspaper or brown paper, and perhaps he didn't carry them in a bag but in a basket, covered with a dishcloth, for hygienic and aesthetic and even practical reasons. And addressing that roomful of smiling southern professors, Nicanor Parra evoked the old University of Concepción, which was probably disappearing into the void, and continues to disappear, even now, into the void's inertia or our perception of it; and he remembered his younger self: badly dressed, we can assume, wearing sandals and the ill-fitting clothes of a poor adolescent, and everything—even the smell of that time, a smell of Chilean colds and southern flus—was trapped like a butterfly by the question that Wittgenstein asks himself and us, speaking from another time, from faraway Europe, a question to which there is no answer: Is *this* hand a hand or isn't it?

Latin America was Europe's mental asylum just as North America was its factory. The foremen have taken over the factory now and the labor force is made up of escapees from the asylum. For over sixty years, the asylum has been burning in its own oil, its own fat.

Today I read an interview with a famous and shrewd Latin American author. They ask him to name three people he admires. He replies: Nelson Mandela, Gabriel García Márquez, and Mario Vargas Llosa. With that answer as a starting point, you could write a whole thesis about the current state of Latin American literature. The casual reader might wonder what links those three figures. There is something that links two of them: the Nobel Prize. And there is something more that links all three: years ago they were all left-wing. They probably all admire the voice of Miriam Makeba. All three have probably danced to her catchy hit song "Pata Pata," García Márquez and Vargas Llosa in colorful Latin American apartments, Mandela in the solitude of his prison cell. All three have made way for deplorable heirs: the clear and entertaining epigones of García Márquez and Vargas Llosa, and, in the case of Mandela, the indescribable Thabo Mbeki, the current president of South Africa, who denies the existence of AIDS. How could anyone name those three, without batting an eyelid, as the figures he most admires? Why not Bush, Putin, and Castro? Why not Mullah Omar, Haider, and Berlusconi? Why not Sánchez Dragó, Sánchez Dragó, and Sánchez Dragó, disguised as the Holy Trinity?

•

Declarations like that are a sign of the times. Of course, I'm prepared to do whatever's necessary (though that sounds unnecessarily melodramatic) to ensure that the shrewd writer in question remains free to make that declaration or any other, according to his taste and inclinations—to ensure that everyone can say what they want to say and write what they want to write and publish it as well. I'm against censorship and self-censorship. But on one condition, as Alcaeus of Mytilene said: if you're going to say what you want to say, you're going to hear what you don't want to hear.

The fact is, Latin American literature isn't Borges or Macedonio Fernández or Onetti or Bioy or Cortázar or Rulfo or Revueltas or even that pair of old bucks García Márquez and Vargas Llosa. Latin American literature is Isabel Allende, Luis Sepúlveda, Ángeles Mastretta, Sergio Ramírez, Tomás Eloy Martínez, a certain Aguilar Camín or Comín, and many other illustrious names that escape me for the moment.

The work of Reinaldo Arenas is already lost. And the work of Puig, Copi, Roberto Arlt. No one reads Ibargüengoitia anymore. Monterroso, who might well have included Mandela, García Márquez, and Vargas Llosa in his list of unforgettable figures (though maybe he would have replaced Vargas Llosa with Bryce Echenique), will soon be swallowed up by the mechanism of oblivion. This is the age of the writer as civil servant, the writer as thug, the writer as gym rat, the writer who goes to Houston or the Mayo Clinic in New York for medical treatment. Vargas Llosa never gave a better lesson in literature than when he went jogging at the crack of dawn. And García Márquez never taught us more than when he welcomed the pope in Havana, wearing patent leather boots—García, not the pope, who I guess would have been wearing sandals—along with Castro, who was booted too. I can still remember the smile that García Márquez was not quite able to contain on that grand occasion. Half-closed eyes, taut skin as if he'd just had a face-lift, slightly puckered lips, Saracen lips, as Amado Nervo would have said, green with envy.

What can Sergio Pitol, Fernando Vallejo, and Ricardo Piglia do to counter the avalanche of glamour? Not much. They can write. But writing and literature are worthless if they aren't accompanied by something more imposing than mere survival. Literature, especially in Latin America, and I suspect in Spain as well, means success, by which, of course, I mean social success: massive print runs; translations into more than thirty languages (I can name twenty languages, but beyond twenty-five I run into trouble, not because I doubt that language number twenty-six exists, but because it's hard for me to imagine the Burmese publishing industry or Burmese readers quivering with emotion at the magical-realist escapades of Eva Luna); a house in New York or Los Angeles; dinners with the rich and famous (as a result of which we learn that Bill Clinton can recite whole paragraphs of *Huckleberry Finn* by heart, or that President Aznar reads Cernuda); making the cover of *Newsweek* and landing six-figure advances.

•

Writers today, as Pere Gimferrer would be quick to point out, are no longer young men of means unafraid to inveigh against the norms of respectable society, much less a bunch of misfits, but products of the middle and working classes determined to scale the Everest of respectability, hungry for respectability. Blond- and dark-haired children of Madrid, born into the lower-middle class and hoping to end their days on the next rung up. They don't reject respectability. They pursue it desperately. And in order to attain it they really have to sweat. They have to sign books, smile, travel to unfamiliar places, smile, make fools of themselves on celebrity talk shows, keep on smiling, never, never bite the hand that feeds them, participate in literary festivals and reply good-humoredly to the most moronic questions, smile in the most appalling situations, look intelligent, control population growth, and always say thank you.

It's hardly surprising that they are prone to sudden fatigue. The struggle for respectability is exhausting. But the new writers had and in some cases still have parents (may God preserve them for many years to come), parents who exhausted themselves, who wore themselves out for a manual laborer's paltry wages, and as a result the new writers know that there are things in life far more exhausting than smiling incessantly and saying yes to the powerful. Of course there are far more exhausting things. And there's something touching about their efforts to secure a place in the pastures of respectability, although it means elbowing others aside. There are no more heroes like Aldana, who said, Now it is time to die, but there are professional pundits and talk show guests, there are members of the academy and political party animals (on the left and the right), there are cunning plagiarists, seasoned social climbers, Machiavellian cowards, figures who would not be out of place in earlier ages of literary history, and who, in the face of numerous obstacles, play their parts, often with a certain elegance—and they are precisely the writers that we, the readers or the viewers or the public (the public, the public, as Margarita Xirgu whispered into García Lorca's ear) deserve.

God bless Hernán Rivera Letelier, God bless his schmaltz, his sentimentality, his politically correct opinions, his clumsy formal tricks, since I am partly responsible. God bless the idiot children of García Márquez and the idiot children of Octavio Paz, since I am to blame for them seeing the light. God bless Fidel Castro's concentration camps for homosexuals and the twenty thousand who disappeared in Argentina and Videla's puzzled mug and Perón's old macho grin projected into the sky and the child killers of Rio de Janeiro and Hugo Chávez's Spanish which smells of shit and is shit, since I created it.

Everything is folklore in the end. We're good at fighting and lousy in bed. Or was it the other way round, Maquieira? I can't remember anymore. Fuguet is right: you have to land those fellowships and massive advances. You have to sell yourself before the buyers (whoever they are) lose interest. The last

Latin Americans who knew who Jacques Vaché was were Julio Cortázar and Mario Santiago, and both of them are dead. The story of Penélope Cruz in India is worthy of our most illustrious stylists. Pe arrives in India. Since she likes local color or authenticity she goes to eat in one of the worst restaurants in Calcutta or Bombay. Pe's own words. One of the worst or one of the cheapest or one of the most down-market places. She sees a hungry little boy at the door who stares back at her fixedly. Pe gets up, goes out, and asks the boy what's wrong. The boy asks her for a glass of milk. Which is odd, because Pe isn't drinking milk. Nevertheless, the actress gets a glass of milk and takes it to the boy, who is waiting patiently at the door. He gulps the glass of milk straight down, under Pe's benevolent gaze. When the boy finishes the glass, Pe tells us, his grateful happy smile makes her think of all the things she has but doesn't need, although Pe is wrong there, because in fact she needs everything she has, absolutely everything. A few days later, Pe has a long philosophical but also practical conversation with Mother Teresa of Calcutta. At one point she tells the story of the boy. She talks about the necessary and the superfluous, about being and not-being, about being-in-relation-to and not-being-in-relation-with . . . what? How does it work? And in the end what does it mean "to be"? To be oneself? Pe gets confused. Meanwhile Mother Teresa keeps moving like a rheumatic weasel around the room or the porch where they're talking, while the Calcutta sun, the balmy sun, but also the sun of the living dead, scatters its dying rays, as it sinks away in the west. Yes, yes, says Mother Teresa and then she murmurs something that Pe doesn't understand. What? asks Pe in English. Be yourself. Don't worry about fixing the world, says Mother Teresa: help, help, help one person, give a glass of milk to one child, and that will be enough, sponsor one child, just one, and that will be enough, says Mother Teresa in Italian, clearly in a bad mood. When night falls, Pe returns to her hotel. She takes a shower, changes her clothes, dabs herself with perfume, all the while unable to forget Mother Teresa's words. When dessert is served: suddenly—illumination! It's all a matter of taking a tiny pinch out of your savings. It's all a matter of not getting distressed. Give an Indian child twelve thousand pesetas a year and you're already doing something. And don't get distressed and don't feel guilty. Don't smoke, eat dried fruit, and don't feel guilty. Thrift and goodness are indissolubly linked.

A number of enigmas are still floating in the air like ectoplasm. If Pe went to eat in a cheap restaurant, why didn't she end up with a case of gastroenteritis? And why did Pe, who isn't short of money, go to a cheap restaurant in the first place? To save money?

We're lousy in bed, lousy at braving the elements, but good at saving. We hoard everything. As if we knew the asylum was going to burn down. We hide everything. The treasures that Pizarro will return to rob over and over again, but also utterly useless things: junk, loose threads, letters, buttons, which we stash in places that are then wiped from our memories, because our memories are weak. And yet we like to keep, to hoard, to save. If we could, we'd save ourselves for better times. We're lost without mom and dad. Although we suspect that mom and dad made us ugly and stupid and bad so they could shine by contrast in the eyes of posterity. Saving, for mom and dad, meant permanence, work, and a pantheon, while for us, saving is about success, money, and respectability. We're only interested in success, money, and respectability. We are the middle-class generation.

Permanence has been swept aside by the rapidity of empty images. The pantheon, we discover to our astonishment, is the doghouse of the burning asylum.

If we could crucify Borges, we would. We are the fearful killers, the careful killers. We think our brain is a marble mausoleum, when in fact it's a house made of cardboard boxes, a shack stranded between an empty field and an endless dusk. (And, anyway, who's to say that we didn't crucify Borges? Borges said as much by dying in Geneva.)

And so let us do as García Márquez bids and read Alexandre Dumas. Let us follow the advice of Pérez Dragó or García Conte and read Pérez-Reverte. The reader (and by the same token the publishing industry) will find salvation in the bestseller. Who would have thought. All that carrying on about

Proust, all those hours spent examining pages of Joyce suspended on a wire, and the answer was there all along, in the bestseller. Ah, the bestseller. But we're lousy in bed and we'll probably put our foot in it again. Everything suggests that there is no way out of this.

PERMISSION ACKNOWLEDGMENTS

Translator's Note: The epigraph to the book is taken from Edwin and Willa Muir's translation of Franz Kafka's "Josephine the Singer, or The Mouse People" (in *Selected Stories of Franz Kafka*, Modern Library, New York, 1952). The translation of "Brise Marine" ("Sea Breeze") by Stéphane Mallarmé in "Literature + Illness = Illness" is by E. H. and A. M. Blackmore, and is quoted from *Six French Poets of the Nineteenth Century* (Oxford, Oxford University Press, 2000). The translation of "Le Voyage" ("Travelers") by Charles Baudelaire in "Literature + Illness = Illness" is by Richard Howard, and is quoted from *Les fleurs du mal: The Complete Text of "The Flowers of Evil"* (London, Picador, 1987). In "The Myths of Cthulhu," "Hear this. To the right hand side of the routine signpost (coming—of course—from north-northwest), right where a bored skeleton yawns" is a slightly modified version of Andrew Hurley's translation of some lines of poetry in Jorge Luis Borges's story "The Aleph" (in *Collected Fictions*, Viking, New York, 1998).

Grateful acknowledgment is made to *Harper's Magazine*, *The New Yorker*, and *Zoetrope*, where some of this material first appeared.